ID0464853

A Wedding Gift

AND OTHER ANGLING STORIES

JOHN TAINTOR FOOTE was born in Leadville, Colorado, in 1881 and died in Hollywood in 1950. He is best known for sophisticated and affectionate stories about the worlds of fly fishing ("A Wedding Gift," "Fatal Gesture"), hunting dogs ("Dumb-Bell of Brookfield," "Pocono Shot") and horse racing ("Shame on You," "The Look of Eagles"). But he also wrote two satiric comedies, *Toby's Bow* and *Tight Britches*, that played on Broadway, and a number of short novels *(Full Personality)* and shorter fiction on wide-ranging subjects that often appeared in the old *Saturday Evening Post.*

In the late 1930s he went to Hollywood to turn *The Look of Eagles* into a celebrated film, *Kentucky*, with Walter Brennan and Loretta Young, that is often re-run today. Thereafter he wrote film scripts, eventually becoming a writer-producer. Among his credits after *Kentucky* were *The Story of Seabiscuit* and *The Mark of Zorro.*

A WEDDING GIFT

AND OTHER ANGLING STORIES

John Taintor Foote

WITH SPECIAL INTRODUCTIONS AND A NEW STORY BY

Timothy Foote

 LYONS & BURFORD, PUBLISHERS

THE HANDSOME LINE DRAWINGS ARE BY

Gordon Allen

The special contents of this edition, including the Introduction, the notes to each story, all stories, and "The Loch Ness Monster" © 1992 by Timothy Foote. Illustrations © 1992 By Gordon Allen. "A Wedding Gift" © 1923 by Curtis Publishing Company, © 1924 by D. Appleton & Company, © 1947 by John Taintor Foote. "Fatal Gesture" © 1933 by John Taintor Foote; renewal © 1961 by Jessie T. Foote. "Daughter of Delilah" © 1936 by Curtis Publishing Company; renewal © 1964 by Jessie T. Foote.

All rights reserved. No part of this book may be reproduced without the express written consent of the publisher, except in the case of brief excerpts in critical reviews and articles. All inquiries should be addressed to Lyons & Burford, Publishers, 31 West 21 Street, New York, New York 10010.

Typesetting by Fisher Composition, Inc.
Printed in the United States of America
10 9 8 7 6 5 4 3 2 1
Text design by Liz Driesbach

Library of Congress Cataloging-in-Publication Data
Foote, John Taintor, 1881-1950.
    A wedding gift, and other angling stories / John Taintor
Foote : with special introductions and a new story by Timothy
Foote.
        p. cm.
    Contents: A wedding gift—Fatal gesture—Daughter of
Delilah—The Loch Ness monster.
    ISBN 1-55821-163-2 : $16.95
    1. Fishing stories, American. I. Foote, Timothy. II. Title.
PS3511.0345W44 1992
813'.52—dc20   91-46263
                                                        CIP

CONTENTS

INTRODUCTION

I was nine years old when my father gave me my first trout rod. It came from Abercrombie & Fitch, a beautiful 3⅜ ounce three-piece Thomas Special. The scene was ready-made for a story. There was I, a twerpish little kid living on the banks of the Beaverkill. And there was my father, a fly fisherman of some renown about to head for darkest Hollywood, never to return. (He was going to turn one of his stories into the movie that became *Kentucky*.) Between us, then as now, was that magic little rod with its two tips, one so fine a mouse would scarcely dare put it to use, its green drill bag and beautifully machined metal case exuding an elixir aroma of varnish and fishing that half a century has not diminished. It was a lifetime's key to the world of trout.

Since then I've ruined a couple of bamboo trout rods, mostly at the rough business of taking smallmouth bass in streams with bucktails and poppers. The age of glass and graphite eventually rolled over me as well, producing a rod made by my friend and editor Don Moser that helped my control and distance a good deal. But over the intervening years, except for some tours of duty in France, I've carefully used the Thomas a time or two on the Beaverkill every summer. Just unscrewing the cap of its case is a ticket to memories that years mostly spent in cities as a magazine writer and editor happily do not erase.

The same is true of my father's George Baldwin Potter stories collected here. Year after year I reread them. Year after year they make me laugh out loud. And for more than a half century now, in all sorts of odd corners of the world, I've met up with folk who know them, some who have given copies away to friends, some who have just stumbled across them. For many of them, as for me, George Baldwin Potter seems to be as real as a Dark Hendrickson.

All three stories are marked by an affectionate knowledge of fly fishing, but they are stories, not articles disguised as stories. They have nothing to do with things like matching the hatch or how to cast an upstream loop so your fly will float a second longer without drag. They are comedies of character, worldly-wise and often sophisticated-funny. Partly because they all involve blithe skirmishing in the war between the sexes, they remind me of the best light-hearted film comedies of the 1930s. At issue in George Baldwin Potter's case, of course, is the timeless, tragical-comical tension that exists between husbands who fish and wives who do not.

Storytellers put to use (and distort) in their fiction whatever comes to hand from real life, and inevitably there is some lore behind these stories. Who was the woman in John Taintor Foote's most famous fishing story, "A Wedding Gift"? Who, for that matter, was the prototype of George Baldwin Potter, worshipper of priceless "Spinoza" rods and relentless proselytizer for the dry fly in fast water?

Fiction being what it is, there is no answer to such questions. But, especially for me, there are intriguing hints and guesses. With my father long dead and my mother recently departed this life in Beaverkill at age ninety-five, I probably know more about John Taintor Foote's stories than anyone in the world. A certain amount of personal background, as well as some biographical speculations are offered in the individual introductions to the stories in this book. One of the funnier lines from "A Wedding Gift," for example, occurs when fashionable Isabelle, hijacked into the Maine woods for her honeymoon, refuses to wear the dumpy, hand-me-down fishing clothes George assembles for her. "I wouldn't let a fish see me looking like that," she says. The remark (one can easily imagine Irene Dunne delivering it) is supposed to have originated under somewhat similar conditions with the new bride of imperious Edward Ringwood Hewitt, creator of the Hewitt nymph and a tireless student of trout.

Everybody who reads and fishes for a certain number of years acquires an informal anthology that lives in affectionate private memory, occasionally reinforced by taking this or that volume down off the shelves for a reread. Perhaps inevitably, my own starts with the George Baldwin Potter stories—especially, for rather personal reasons, "Daughter of Delilah." But it also includes such things as Arthur Train's "Mr. Tutt's Revenge," in which Ephraim Tutt, complete with stogie and stovepipe hat, gets his own back from a snooty Canadian fishing club for insult and injury on the stream. Frederick Van de Water's "Trout and the Old Gentleman" has always pleased me, but to any man over fifty his courtly and compelling fable about the dangers of putting off fishing in favor of work really strikes home. (Some of these literary enthusiasms, it will be seen, drifted into the story of my own that is used to close out this collection.)

Recent writers tend to use less satiric and outrageous caricature than was my father's fashion. They deal more seriously with life and fishing in subtle and sophisticated contexts. I think particularly of Nick Lyons' "The Legacy," in which the sale of a dead man's fishing gear somberly evokes not only a whole life but a clash of generations and cultures that cuts to the heart. And of course, everyone's favorite fishing novel is *A River Runs Through It*, Norman Maclean's peerless account of his brother's life and death in Montana, transmogrified into an indulgent fiction that has acquired a readership among people who do not fish.

Nine of John Taintor Foote's stories were collected in *Anglers All* some forty-five years ago. In 1958, "A Wedding Gift" appeared (beside William Faulkner's "The Bear" and not far from the wolf-hunting scene from Tolstoy's *War and Peace*!) in a *Sports Illustrated* collection of great sports stories. My father died eight years before the book came out but he would have been pleased by such company, as I was for him. Now and then individual stories have turned up in anthologies ever since. But it seems time to offer the best of them again.

One reason (anyone who has been involved with book publishing knows this) is that you have to keep reintroducing books and people, even books you figure everybody must have read long ago. How often it turns out that they haven't.

5

Another, clearly, is the change that has taken place in fly fishing itself. Once the arcane sport of the happy few, it has spread by leaps and bounds, creating legions of avid equipment experts, antique rod collectors, folks who matriculate at fly-fishing schools, many of them interested not only in fishing but in the accumulating lore of the sport. These enormous changes have left me behind; I read the ads for antique rods, glance through the catalogues, talk to friends far more knowledgeable than I, but still fish with only a few patterns, mostly with a shortish line in riffled water. (George Baldwin Potter, at least, would approve.)

Not long ago on the Beaverkill, though, the broadening interest was brought home to me, and with it the conviction that this collection might be overdue. It was late in the day and I was just starting in to put a fly at the head of a stretch of water we used to call Marble's Pool, when a young man, less than half my age I'd guess, stopped his car on the road nearby and walked over. This was private water and, not knowing me, he was checking things out. I cited the right name. There was a pause. He looked at me and my rod. "You're using an F. E. Thomas Special," he said.

He was right. But at that distance in that (or any other) light how could he tell? And for an instant I wondered why in the world he would care enough to learn that much about trout-rod taxonomy in the first place? But for collectors and aficionados any working antique is the bread of life. The rod my father gave me more than fifty years ago is still full of life. So are his stories.

Beaverkill, N.Y.
Spring 1991

6

A Wedding Gift

*IN MY PARENTS' HOUSE IN BEAVERKILL, ON A SHELF HALFWAY UP
a dark stairway where no one could possibly see it without a
flashlight, sits a vast, hand-painted serving dish. Gold-trimmed,
blue-bordered, nearly thirty inches long and with a huge trout
swirling up out of its center at an artificial fly, it is a fairly
horrendous object. No one ever mentioned it in the family when I
was young, but anyone seeing it who has read "A Wedding Gift"
will have no trouble identifying the source of the fancy fish plates
presented to George Baldwin Potter as the wedding present that give
the story its title—and its closing lines.*

*"A Wedding Gift" is the story of a hellish but funny honeymoon
in a remote fishing camp. First published in 1923, only a few years
after my parents were married, it introduces George and Isabelle, a
decorous but warring couple whose doings preoccupied my father in
print off and on for a decade.*

*My parents were neither of them much given to speaking about
personal things. By 1928 my mother had learned to fish, but as a
child I gradually came to understand that among the rankling early
milestones of a difficult marriage was some kind of astonishing
quarrel in a backwoods fishing camp. In retrospect I came to realize
that apart from a fondness for Kipling and the theater, for the
outdoors and for having a big house in the country, like George and
Isabelle they soon began to disagree dramatically about all sorts of
things, notably about antiques and matters of taste in the furnishing
of a big house in the country. Including, I have no doubt, a certain
set of hand-painted, trout-decorated china.*

Beyond that, such correspondences as there may, or may not be, between life and art are notably ambiguous. Unlike Isabelle, who is a drawing-room-comedy caricature, my mother was no incipient suburban matron. She was a girl who had camped out (and taught school) in the hills of British Columbia, got herself through Berkeley and so to Broadway where she played the ingenue lead in a play called Toby's Bow by John Taintor Foote, and thereafter married the playwright. Like Isabelle, however, she was reckoned a beauty, had no shortage of temperament, and was many years younger than her husband. My father, like George, was forty when he married. An interested student of literature and life may make of that what he will.

When "A Wedding Gift" was anthologized by Sports Illustrated in 1958, the editors noted that, except for the reference to a hip flask, the story had not dated at all in nearly forty years. Rereading it after nearly forty more, I think that judgment still pretty well applies—except for George's "shocking" language to Isabelle during the fight with the Great Trout, which no classic fishing story used to do without.

Very late in her life I dared ask my mother about that moment in the story. Had she ever been gathering greenery and wild flowers by a big pool where my father was fishing and failed to net a big fish? (To preserve the suspense I disguise the true horror of Isabelle's actual act.)

To my surprise she nodded "Yes." And added rather defensively, "I didn't know anything about fishing then."

"What did he say?" I asked.

"He said, 'Go to H——!'"

At the time, using such language on a woman was officially unforgivable, and Isabelle, who got the same treatment, is predictably outraged. Nowadays, with the air practically blue with four-letter words, even around young girls, I wonder if a modern reader will credit Isabelle's shock and extreme umbrage. But then, as any husband learns (and George admits), in marriage it is the tone, not the words, that seem to matter most.

George Baldwin Potter is a purist. That is to say, he either takes trout on a dry fly or he does not take them at all. He belongs to a number of fishing clubs, any member of which might acquire his neighbor's wife, beat his children or poison a dog and still cast a fly, in all serenity, upon club waters; but should he impale on a hook a lowly though succulent worm and immerse the creature in those same waters it would be better that he send in his resignation at once, sooner than face the shaken committee that would presently wait upon him.

George had become fixed in my mind as a bachelor. This, of course, was a mistake. I am continually forgetting that purists rush into marriage when approaching or having just passed the age of forty. The psychology of this is clear.

For twenty years, let us say, a purist's life is completely filled by his efforts to convert all reasonable men to his own particular method of taking trout. He thinks, for example, that a man should not concern himself with more than a dozen types of standard flies. The manner of presenting them is the main consideration. Take any one of these flies, then, and place it, by means of an eight-foot rod, a light, tapered line and a mist-colored leader of reasonable length, on fast water—if you want trout. Of course, if you want to listen to the birds and look at the scenery, fish the pools with a long line and a twelve-foot leader. Why, it stands to reason that—

The years go by as he explains these vital facts patiently, again and again, to Smith and Brown and Jones. One wet, cold spring, after fighting a muddy stream all day, he reexplains for the better part of an evening and takes himself, somewhat wearily, upstairs. The damp and chill of the room at whatever club he may be fishing is positively tomb-like. He can hear the rain drumming on the roof and swishing against the windows. The water will be higher than ever tomorrow, he reflects, as he puts out the lights and slides between the icy sheets. Steeped to the soul in cheerless dark, he recalls numbly that when he first met Smith and Brown and Jones they were fishing the pools with a long line. That was, let's see—fifteen—eighteen—twenty years ago. Then he must be forty. It isn't possible! Yes, it is a fact. It is also a fact that Smith and Brown and Jones are still fishing the pools with a long line.

In the first faint light of dawn he falls into an uneasy, muttering slumber. The dark hours between have been devoted to intense thought and a variety of wiggles which have not succeeded in keeping the bedclothes against his shoulder blades.

Some time within the next six months you will remember that you have forgotten to send him a wedding present.

George, therefore, having arrived at his fortieth birthday, announced his engagement shortly thereafter. Quite by chance I ran across his bride-to-be and himself a few days before the ceremony, and joined them at lunch. She was a blonde in the early twenties, with wide blue eyes and a typical rose-and-white complexion. A rushing, almost breathless account of herself, which she began the moment we were seated, was curious, I thought. It was as though she feared an interruption at any moment. I learned that she was an only child, born and reared in Greater New York; that her family had recently moved to New Rochelle; that she had been shopping madly for the past two weeks; that she was nearly dead, but she had some adorable things.

At this point George informed me that they would spend their honeymoon at a certain fishing club in Maine. He then proceeded to describe the streams and lakes in that section at some length—during the rest of the luncheon, as a matter of fact. His fiancée, who had fallen into a wordless abstraction, only broke her silence with a vague murmur as we parted.

Owing to this meeting I did not forget to send a wedding present. I determined that my choice should please both George and his wife through the happy years to come.

If I had had George only to consider, I could have settled the business in two minutes at a sporting-goods store. Barred from these for obvious reasons, I spent a long day in a thoroughly exhausting search. Late in the afternoon I decided to abandon my hopeless task. I had made a tremendous effort and failed. I would simply buy a silver doodab and let it go at that.

As I staggered into a store with the above purpose in view, I passed a show case devoted to fine china, and halted as my eyes fell on a row of fish plates backed by artfully rumpled blue velvet. The plates proved to be hand painted. On each plate was one of the different varieties of trout, curving up through green depths to an artificial fly just dropping on the surface of the water.

In an automatic fashion I indicated the plates to a clerk, paid for them, gave him my card and the address and fled from the store. Some time during the next twenty-four hours it came to me that George Potter was not among my nearest and dearest. Yet the unbelievable sum I had left with that clerk in exchange for those fish plates could be justified in no other way.

I thought this fact accounted for the sort of frenzy with which George flung himself upon me when next we met, some two months later. I had been week-ending in the country and encountered him in the Grand Central Station as I emerged from the lower level. For a long moment he wrung my hand in silence, gazing almost feverishly into my face. At last he spoke:

"Have you got an hour to spare?"

It occurred to me that it would take George an hour at least to describe his amazed delight at the splendor of my gift. The clock above Information showed that it was 12:45. I therefore suggested that we lunch together.

He, too, glanced at the clock, verified its correctness by his watch and seized me by the arm.

"All right," he agreed, and was urging me toward the well-filled and somewhat noisy station café before I grasped his intention and tried to suggest that we go elsewhere. His hand only tightened on my arm.

"It's all right," he said; "good food, quick service—you'll like it."

He all but dragged me into the café and steered me to a table in the corner. I lifted my voice above an earnest clatter of gastronomical utensils and made a last effort.

"The Biltmore's just across the street."

George pressed me into my chair, shoved a menu card at me and addressed the waiter.

"Take his order." Here he jerked out his watch and consulted it again. "We have forty-eight minutes. Service for one. I shan't eat anything; or, no—bring me some coffee—large cup—black."

Having ordered mechanically, I frankly stared at George. He was dressed, I now observed, with unusual care. He wore a rather dashing gray suit. His tie, which was an exquisite shade of gray-blue, was embellished by a handsome pearl. The handkerchief, appearing above his breast pocket, was of the same delicate gray-blue shade as the tie. His face had been recently and closely shaven, also powdered; but above that smooth whiteness of jowl was a pair of curiously glittering eyes and a damp, a beaded brow. This he now mopped with his napkin.

"Good God," said I, "what is it, George?"

His reply was to extract a letter from his inside coat pocket and pass it across the table, his haunted eyes on mine. I took in its few lines at a glance:

> Father has persuaded me to listen to what you call your explanation. I arrive Grand Central 1:45, daylight saving, Monday.
>
> ISABELLE

Poor old George, I thought; some bachelor indiscretion; and now, with his honeymoon scarcely over, blackmail, a lawsuit, heaven only knew what.

"Who," I asked, returning the letter, "is Isabelle?"

To my distress, George again resorted to his napkin. Then, "My wife," he said.

"Your wife!"

George nodded.

"Been living with her people for the last month. Wish he'd bring that coffee. You don't happen to have a flask with you?"

"Yes, I have a flask." George brightened. "But it's empty. Do you want to tell me about your trouble? Is that why you brought me here?"

"Well, yes," George admitted. "But the point is—will you stand by me? That's the main thing. She gets in"—here he consulted his watch—"in forty-five minutes, if the train's on time." A sudden panic seemed to seize him. His hand shot across the table and grasped my wrist. "You've got to stand by me, old man—until the ice is broken. That's all I ask. Just stick until the train gets in. Then act as if you knew nothing. Say you ran into me here and stayed to meet her. I'll tell you what—say I didn't seem to want you to stay. Kid me about wanting her all to myself, or something like that. Get the point? It'll give me a chance to sort of—well, you understand."

"I see what you mean, of course," I admitted. "Here's your coffee. Suppose you have some and then tell me what this is all about—if you care to, that is."

"No sugar, no cream," said George to the waiter; "just pour it. Don't stand there waving it about—pour it, pour it!" He attempted to swallow a mouthful of steaming coffee, gurgled frightfully and grabbed his water glass. "Great jumping Jehoshaphat!" he gasped, when he could speak, and glared at the waiter, who promptly moved out into the sea of diners and disappeared among a dozen of his kind.

"Steady, George," I advised as I transferred a small lump of ice from my glass to his coffee cup.

George watched the ice dissolve, murmured, "Idiot," several times and presently swallowed the contents of the cup in two gulps.

"I had told her," he said suddenly, "exactly where we were going.

She mentioned Narragansett several times—I'll admit that. Imagine—Narragansett! Of course I bought her fishing things myself. I didn't buy knickers or woolens or flannel shirts—naturally. You don't go around buying a girl breeches and underwear before you're married. It wouldn't be—well, it isn't done, that's all. I got her the sweetest three-ounce rod you ever held in your hand. I'll bet I could put out sixty feet of line with it against the wind. I got her a pair of English waders that didn't weigh a pound. They cost me forty-five dollars. The rest of the outfit was just as good. Why, her fly box was a Truxton. I could have bought an American imitation for eight dollars. I know a lot of men who'll buy leaders for themselves at two dollars apiece and let their wives fish with any kind of tackle. I'll give you my word I'd have used anything I got her myself. I sent it all out to be packed with her things. I wanted her feel that it was her own—not mine. I know a lot of men who give their wives a high-class rod or an imported reel and then fish with it themselves. What time is it?"

"Clock right up there," I said. But George consulted his watch and used his napkin distressingly again.

"Where was I?"

"You were telling me why you sent her fishing things out to her."

"Oh, yes! That's all of that. I simply wanted to show you that from the first I did all any man could do. Ever been in the Cuddiwink district?"

I said that I had not.

"You go in from Buck's Landing. A lumber tug takes you up to the head of Lake Owonga. Club guides meet you there and put you through in one day—twenty miles by canoe and portage up the west branch of the Penobscot; then nine miles by trail to Lost Pond. The club's on Lost Pond. Separate cabins, with a main dining and loafing camp, and the best squaretail fishing on earth—both lake and stream. Of course, I don't fish the lakes. A dry fly belongs on a stream and nowhere else. Let me make it perfectly clear."

George's manner suddenly changed. He hunched himself closer to the table, dropped an elbow upon it and lifted an expository finger.

"The dry fly," he stated, with a new almost combative ring in his voice, "is designed primarily to simulate not only the appearance of the natural insect but its action as well. This action is arrived at through the flow of the current. The moment you move a fly by means of a leader you destroy the—"

I saw that an interruption was imperative.

"Yes, of course," I said; "but your wife will be here in—"

It was pitiful to observe George. His new-found assurance did not flee—flee suggests a withdrawal, however swift—it was immediately and totally annihilated. He attempted to pour himself some coffee, take out his watch, look at the clock and mop his brow with his napkin at one and the same instant.

"You were telling me how to get to Lost Pond," I suggested.

"Yes, to be sure," said George. "Naturally you go in light. The things you absolutely have to have—rods, tackle, waders, wading shoes, and so forth, are about all a guide can manage at the portages in addition to the canoe. You pack in extras yourself—change of underclothes, a couple of pairs of socks and a few toilet articles. You leave a bag or trunk at Buck's Landing. I explained this to her. I explained it carefully. I told her either a week-end bag or one small trunk. Herb Trescott was my best man. I left everything to him. He saw us on the train and handed me tickets and reservations just before we pulled out. I didn't notice in the excitement of getting away that he'd given me three trunk checks all stamped 'Excess.' I didn't notice it till the conductor showed up, as a matter of fact. Then I said, 'Darling, what in heaven's name have you brought three trunks for?' She said—I can remember her exact words—'Then you're not going to Narragansett?'

"I simply looked at her. I was too dumbfounded to speak. At last I pulled myself together and told her that in three days we'd be whipping the best squaretail water in the world. I took her hand, I remember, and said, 'You and I together, sweetheart,' or something like that."

George sighed and lapsed into a silence which remained unbroken until his eye happened to encounter the face of the clock. He started and went on:

"We got to Buck's Landing, by way of Bangor, at six in the evening of the following day. Buck's Landing is a railroad station with grass growing between the ties, a general store and hotel combined, and a lumber wharf. The store keeps canned peas, pink-and-white-candy and felt boots. The hotel part is—well, it doesn't matter except that I don't think I ever saw so many deer heads; a few stuffed trout, but mostly deer heads. After supper the proprietor and I got the three trunks up to the largest room. We just got them in and that was all. The tug left for the head of the lake at seven next morning. I explained this to Isabelle. I said we'd leave the trunks there until we came out, and offered to help her unpack the one her fishings things were in. She said, 'Please go away!' So I went. I got out a rod and went down to the wharf. No trout there, I knew; but I thought I'd limber up my wrist. I put on a Cahill Number Fourteen—or was it Sixteen—"

George knitted his brows and stared intently but unseeingly at me for some little time.

"Call it a Sixteen," I suggested.

George shook his head impatiently and remained concentrated in thought.

"I'm inclined to think it was a Fourteen," he said at last. "But let it go; it'll come to me later. At any rate, the place was alive with big chub—a foot long, some of 'em. I'll bet I took fifty—threw 'em back, of course. They kept on rising after it got dark. I'd tell myself I'd go after one more cast. Each time I'd hook a big chub, and—well, you know how the time slips away.

"When I got back to the hotel all the lights were out. I lit matches until I got upstairs and found the door to the room. I'll never forget what I saw when I opened that door—never! Do you happen to know how many of the kind of things they wear a woman can get into one trunk? Well, she had three and she'd unpacked them all. She had used the bed for the gowns alone. It was piled with them—literally piled; but that wasn't a starter. Everywhere you looked was a stack of things with ribbons in 'em. There were enough shoes and stockings for a girls'

school; silk stockings, mind you, and high-heeled shoes and slippers."
Here George consulted clock and watch. "I wonder if that train's on
time," he wanted to know.

"You have thirty-five minutes, even if it is," I told him; "go right
ahead."

"Well, I could see something was wrong from her face. I didn't know
what, but I started right in to cheer her up. I told her all about the
chub fishing I'd been having. At last she burst into tears. I won't go
into the scene that followed. I'd ask her what was the matter and she'd
say, 'Nothing,' and cry frightfully. I know a lot of men who would have
lost their tempers under the circumstances, but I didn't; I give you my
word. I simply said, 'There, there,' until she quieted down. And that
isn't all. After a while she began to show me her gowns. Imagine—at
eleven o'clock at night, at Buck's Landing! She'd hold up a dress and
look over the top of it at me and ask me how I liked it, and I'd say it
was all right. I know a lot of men who wouldn't have sat there two
minutes.

"At last I said, 'They're all all right, darling,' and yawned. She was
holding up a pink dress covered with shiny dingle-dangles, and she
threw the dress on the bed and all but had hysterics. It was terrible.
In trying to think of some way to quiet her it occurred to me that I'd
put her rod together and let her feel the balance of it with the reel I'd
bought her—a genuine Fleetwood, mind you—attached. I looked
around for her fishing things and couldn't find them. I'll tell you why
I couldn't find them." George paused for an impressive instant to give
his next words the full significance due them. "They weren't there!"

"No?" I murmured weakly.

"No," said George. "And what do you suppose she said when I ques-
tioned her? I can give you her exact words—I'll never forget them. She
said, 'There wasn't any room for them.'" Again George paused. "I ask
you," he inquired at last, "I ask you as man to man; what do you think
of that?"

I found no adequate reply to this question and George, now thoroughly warmed up, rushed on.

"You'd swear I lost my temper then, wouldn't you? Well, I didn't. I did say something to her later, but I'll let you be the judge when we come to that. I'll ask you to consider the circumstances. I'll ask you to get Old Faithful in your mind's eye."

"Old Faithful?" I repeated. "Then you went to the Yellowstone later?"

"Yellowstone! Of course not! Haven't I told you we were already at the best trout water in America? Old Faithful was a squaretail. He'd been in the pool below Horseshoe Falls for twenty years, as a matter of record. We'll come to that presently. How are we off for time?"

"Thirty-one minutes," I told him. "I'm watching the clock—go ahead."

"Well, there she was, on a fishing trip with nothing to fish with. There was only one answer to that—she couldn't fish. But I went over everything she'd brought in three trunks and I'll give you my word she didn't have a garment of any sort you couldn't see through.

"Something had to be done and done quick, that was sure. I fitted her out from my own things with a sweater, a flannel shirt and a pair of knickerbockers. Then I got the proprietor up and explained the situation. He got me some heavy underwear and two pairs of woolen stockings that belonged to his wife. When it came to shoes it looked hopeless, but the proprietor's wife, who had got up, too, by this time, thought of a pair of boy's moccasins that were in the store and they turned out to be about the right size. I made arrangements to rent the room we had until we came out again to keep her stuff in, and took another room for the night—what was left of it after she'd repacked what could stay in the trunks and arranged what couldn't so it wouldn't be wrinkled.

"I got up early, dressed and took my duffel down to the landing. I wakened her when I left the room. When breakfast was ready I went to see why she hadn't come down. She was all dressed, sitting on the edge of the bed. I said, 'Breakfast is ready, darling,' but I saw by her face that something was wrong again. It turned out to be my knickers.

They fitted her perfectly—a little tight in spots—except in the waist. They would simply have fallen off if she hadn't held them up.

"Well, I was going in so light that I only had one belt. The proprietor didn't have any—he used suspenders. Neither did his wife—she used—well, whatever they use. He got me a piece of clothesline and I knotted it at each end and ran it through the what-you-may-call-'ems of the knickers and tied it in front. The knickers sort of puckered all the way round, but they couldn't come down—that was the main thing. I said, 'There you are, darling.' She walked over and tilted the mirror of the bureau so that she could see herself from head to foot. She said, 'Who are going to be at this place where we are going?' I said, 'Some of the very best dry-fly men in the country.' She said, 'I don't mean them; I mean the women. Will there be any women there?'

"I told her, certainly there would be women. I asked her if she thought I would take her into a camp with nothing but men. I named some of the women: Mrs. Fred Beal and Mrs. Brooks Carter and Talcott Ranning's sister and several more.

"She turned around slowly in front of the mirror, staring into it for a minute. Then she said, 'Please go out and close the door.' I said, 'All right, darling; but come right down. The tug will be here in fifteen minutes.'

"I went downstairs and waited ten minutes, then I heard the tug whistle for the landing and ran upstairs again. I knocked at the door. When she didn't answer I went in. Where do you suppose she was?"

I gave it up.

"In bed!" said George in an awe-struck voice. "In bed with her face turned to the wall; and listen, I didn't lose my temper as God is my judge. I rushed down to the wharf and told the tug captain I'd give him twenty-five dollars extra if he'd hold the boat till we came. He said all right and I went back to the room.

"The breeches had done it. She simply wouldn't wear them. I told her that at a fishing camp in Maine clothes were never thought of. I said, 'No one thinks of anything but trout, darling.' She said, 'I wouldn't let a fish see me looking like that.'" George's brow beaded suddenly. His hands dived searchingly into various pockets. "Got a cigarette? I left my case in my other suit."

He took a cigarette from me, lighted it with shaking fingers and inhaled deeply.

"It went on like that for thirty minutes. She was crying all the time, of course. I had started down to tell the tug captain it was all off, and I saw a woman's raincoat hanging in the hall. It belonged to some one up in one of the camps, the proprietor told me. I gave him seventy-five dollars to give to whoever owned it when he came out, and took it upstairs. In about ten minutes I persuaded her to wear it over the rest of her outfit until we got to camp. I told her one of the women would be able to fix her up all right when we got there. I didn't believe it, of course. The women at camp were all old-timers; they'd gone in as light as the men; but I had to say something.

"We had quite a trip going in. The guides were at the head of the lake all right—Indian Joe and a new man I'd never seen, called Charlie. I told Joe to take Isabelle—he's one of the best canoemen I ever saw. I was going to paddle bow for my man, but I'd have bet a cooky Indian Joe could stay with us on any kind of water. We had to beat it right through to make camp by night. It's a good stiff trip, but it can be done. I looked back at the other canoe now and then until we struck about a mile of white water that took all I had. When we were through the other canoe wasn't in sight. The river made a bend there, and I thought it was just behind and would show up any minute.

"Well, it didn't show up and I began to wonder. We hit our first portage about ten o'clock and landed. I watched downstream for twenty minutes, expecting to sight the other canoe every instant. Then Charlie, who hadn't opened his head, said, 'Better go back,' and put the canoe in again. We paddled downstream for all that was in it. I was stiff with fright. We saw 'em coming about three miles lower down and back-paddled till they came up. Isabelle was more cheerful-looking than she'd been since we left New York, but Joe had that stony face an Indian gets when he's sore.

"I said, 'Anything wrong?' Joe just grunted and drove the canoe past us. Then I saw it was filled with wild flowers. Isabelle said she'd been picking them right off the banks all the way along. She said she'd only had to get out of the boat once, for the blue ones. Now, you can't beat that—not in a thousand years. I leave it to you if you can. Twenty miles of stiff current, with five portages ahead of us and a nine-mile hike at the end of that. I gave that Indian the devil for letting her do such a thing, and tipped the flowers into the Penobscot when we un-loaded for the first portage. She didn't speak to me on the portage, and she got into her canoe without a word.

"Nothing more happened going in, except this flower business had lost two hours, and it was so dark when we struck the swamp at Loon Lake that we couldn't follow the trail well and kept stumbling over down timber and stepping into bog holes. She was about fagged out by then, and the mosquitoes were pretty thick through there. Without any warning she sat down in the trail. She did it so suddenly I nearly fell over her. I asked her what was the matter and she said, 'This is the end'—just like that—'this is the end!' I said, 'The end of what, darling?' She said, 'Of everything!' I told her if she sat there all wet and muddy she'd catch her death. She said she hoped so. I said, 'It's only two miles more, darling. Just think, to-morrow we'll be on the best trout water in the world!' With that she said, 'I want my mother, my darling mother,' and bowed her head in her hands. Think it over, please; and remember, I didn't lose my temper. You're sure there's nothing left in your flask?"

"Not a drop, George," I assured him. "Go ahead; we've only twenty-five minutes."

George looked wildly at the clock, then at his watch.

"A man never has it when he wants it most. Have you noticed that? Where was I?"

"You were in the swamp."

"Oh, yes! Well, she didn't speak after that, and nothing I could say would budge her. The mosquitoes had got wind of us when we stopped and were coming in swarms. We'd be eaten alive in another ten minutes. So I told Joe to give his pack to Charlie and help me pick her up and carry her. Joe said, 'No, by damn!' and folded his arms. When an Indian gets sore he stays sore, and when he's sore he's stubborn. The mosquitoes were working on him good and plenty, though, and at last he said, 'Me carry packs. Charlie help carry—that.' He flipped his hand over in the direction of Isabelle and took the pack from Charlie.

"It was black as your hat by now, and the trail through there was only about a foot wide with swamp on each side. It was going to be some job getting her out of there. I thought Charlie and I would make a chair of our arms and stumble along with her some way; but when I started to lift her up she said, 'Don't touch me!' and got up and went on. A blessing if there ever was one. We got to camp at ten that night.

"She was stiff and sore next morning—you expect it after a trip like that—besides, she'd caught a little cold. I asked her how she felt, and she said she was going to die and asked me to send for a doctor and her mother. The nearest doctor was at Bangor and her mother was in New Rochelle. I carried her breakfast over from the dining camp to our cabin. She said she couldn't eat any breakfast, but she did drink a cup of coffee, telling me between sips how awful it was to die alone in a place like that.

"After she'd had the coffee she seemed to feel better. I went to the camp library and got *The Dry Fly on American Waters*, by Charles Darty. I consider him the soundest man in the country. He's better than Pell or Fawcett. My chief criticism of him is that in his chapter on Streams East of the Alleghenies—east of the Alleghenies, mind you—he recommends the Royal Coachman. I consider the Lead-Wing Coachman a serviceable fly on clear, hard-fished water; but the Royal—never! I wouldn't give it a shade over the Professor or the Montreal. Just consider the body alone of the Royal Coachman—never mind the wings and hackle—the body of the Royal is—"

"Yes, I know, George," I said; "but—"

I glanced significantly at the clock. George started, sighed, and resumed his narrative.

"I went back to the cabin and said, 'Darling, here is one of the most intensely interesting books ever written. I'm going to read it aloud to you. I think I can finish it to-day. Would you like to sit up in bed while I read?' She said she hadn't strength enough to sit up in bed, so I sat down beside her and started reading. I had read about an hour, I suppose, when she did sit up in bed quite suddenly. I saw she was staring at me in a queer, wild way that was really startling. I said, 'What is it, darling?' She said, 'I'm going to get up. I'm going to get up this instant.'

"Well, I was delighted, naturally. I thought the book would get her by the time I'd read it through. But there she was, as keen as mustard before I'd got well into it. I'll tell you what I made up my mind to do, right there. I made up my mind to let her use my rod that day. Yes, sir—my three-ounce Spinoza, and what's more, I did it."

George looked at me triumphantly, then lapsed into reflection for a moment.

"If ever a man did everything possible to—well, let it go. The main thing is, I have nothing to reproach myself with—nothing. Except—but we'll come to that presently. Of course, she wasn't ready for dry flies yet. I borrowed some wet flies from the club steward, got some cushions for the canoe and put my rod together. She had no waders, so a stream was out of the question. The lake was better, anyway, that first day; she'd have all the room she wanted for her back cast.

"I stood on the landing with her before we got into the canoe and showed her just how to put out a fly and recover it. Then she tried it." A sort of horror came into George's face. "You wouldn't believe any one could handle a rod like that," he said huskily. "You couldn't believe it unless you'd seen it. Gimme a cigarette.

"I worked with her a half hour or so and saw no improvement—none whatever. At last she said, 'The string is too long. I can't do anything with such a long string on the pole.' I told her gently—gently, mind you—that the string was an eighteen-dollar double-tapered Hurdman line, attached to a Gebhardt reel on a three-ounce Spinoza rod. I said, 'We'll go out on the lake now. If you can manage to get a rise, perhaps it will come to you instinctively.'

"I paddled her out on the lake and she went at it. She'd spat the flies down and yank them up and spat them down again. She hooked me several times with her back cast and got tangled up in the line herself again and again. All this time I was speaking quietly to her, telling her what to do. I give you my word I never raised my voice—not once—and I thought she'd break the tip every moment.

"Finally she said her arm was tired and lowered the rod. She'd got everything messed up with her last cast and the flies were trailing just over the side of the canoe. I said, 'Recover your cast and reel in, darling.' Instead of using her rod, she took hold of the leader close to the flies and started to pull them into the canoe. At that instant a little trout—couldn't have been over six inches—took the tail fly. I don't know exactly what happened, it was all over so quickly. I think she just screamed and let go of everything. At any rate, I saw my Spinoza bounce off the gunwale of the canoe and disappear. There was fifty feet of water just there. And now listen carefully: not one word did I utter—not one. I simply turned the canoe and paddled to the landing in absolute silence. No reproaches of any sort. Think that over!"

I did. My thoughts left me speechless. George proceeded:

"I took out a guide and tried dragging for the rod with a gang hook and heavy sinker all the rest of the day. But the gangs would only foul on the bottom. I gave up at dusk and paddled in. I said to the guide—it was Charlie—I said, 'Well, it's all over, Charlie.' Charlie said, 'I brought Mr. Carter in and he had an extra rod. Maybe you could borrow it. It's a four-ounce Meecham.' I smiled. I actually smiled. I turned and looked at the lake. 'Charlie,' I said, 'somewhere out there in that dark water, where the eye of man will never behold it again, is a three-ounce Spinoza—and you speak of a Meecham.' Charlie said, 'Well, I just thought I'd tell you.' I said, 'That's all right, Charlie. That's all right.' I went to the main camp, saw Jean, the head guide and made arrangements to leave the next day. Then I went to our cabin and sat down before the fire. I heard Isabelle say something about being sorry. I said, 'I'd rather not talk about it, darling. If you don't mind, we'll never mention it again.' We sat there in silence, then, until dinner.

"As we got up from dinner, Nate Griswold and his wife asked us to play bridge with them that evening. I'd told no one what had happened, and Nate didn't know, of course. I simply thanked him and said we were tired, and we went back to our cabin. I sat down before the fire again. Isabelle seemed restless. At last she said, 'George.' I said, 'What is it, darling?' She said, 'Would you like to read to me from that book?' I said, 'I'm sorry, darling; if you don't mind I'll just sit here quietly by the fire.'

"Somebody knocked at the door after a while. I said, 'Come in.' It was Charlie. I said, 'What is it, Charlie?' Then he told me that Bob Frazer had been called back to New York and was going out next morning. I said, 'Well, what of it?' Charlie said, 'I just thought you could maybe borrow his rod.' I said, 'I thought you understood about that, Charlie.' Charlie said, 'Well, that's it. Mr. Frazer's rod is a three-ounce Spinoza.'

"I got up and shook hands with Charlie and gave him five dollars. But when he'd gone I began to realize what was before me. I'd brought in a pint flask of prewar Scotch. Prewar—get that! I put this in my pocket and went over to Bob's cabin. Just as I was going to knock I lost my nerve. I sneaked away from the door and went down to the lake and sat on the steps of the canoe landing. I sat there for quite a while and took several nips. At last I thought I'd just go and tell Bob of my loss and see what he said. I went back to his cabin and this time I knocked. Bob was putting a few odds and ends in a shoulder pack. His rod was in its case, standing against the wall.

"I said, 'I hear you're going out in the morning.' He said, 'Yes, curse it, my wife's mother has to have some sort of a damned operation or other.' I said, 'How would a little drink strike you, Bob?' He said, 'Strike me! Wait a minute! What kind of a drink?' I took out the flask and handed it to him. He unscrewed the cap and held the flask to his nose. He said, 'Great heavens above, it smells like—' I said, 'It is.' He said, 'It can't be!' I said, 'Yes, it is.' He said, 'There's a trick in it somewhere.' I said, 'No, there isn't—I give you my word.' He tasted what was in the flask carefully. Then he said, 'I call this white of you, George,' and took a good stiff snort. When he was handing back the flask he said, 'I'll do as much for you some day, if I ever get the chance.' I took a snifter myself.

"Then I said, 'Bob, something awful has happened to me. I came here to tell you about it.' He said, 'Is that so? Sit down.' I sat down and told him. He said, 'What kind of a rod was it?' I said, 'A three-ounce Spinoza.' He came over and gripped my hand without a word. I said, 'Of course, I can't use anything else.' He nodded, and I saw his eyes flicker toward the corner of the room where his own rod was standing. I said, 'Have another drink, Bob.' But he just sat down and stared at me. I took a good stiff drink myself. Then I said, 'Under ordinary circumstances, nothing on earth could hire me to ask a man to—' I stopped right there.

"Bob got up suddenly and began to walk up and down the room. I said, 'Bob, I'm not considering myself—not for a minute. If it was last season, I'd simply have gone back tomorrow without a word. But I'm not alone any more. I've got the little girl to consider. She's never seen a trout taken in her life—think of it, Bob! And here she is, on her honeymoon, at the best water I know of. On her honeymoon, Bob!' I waited for him to say something, but he went to the window and stared out, with his back to me. I got up and said good night and started for the door. Just as I reached it he turned from the window and rushed over and picked up his rod. He said, 'Here, take it,' and put the rod case in my hands. I started to try to thank him, but he said, 'Just go ahead with it,' and pushed me out the door."

The waiter was suddenly hovering above us with his eyes on the dishes.

"Now what do you want?" said George.

"Never mind clearing here," I said. "Just bring me the check. Go ahead, George."

"Well, of course, I can't any more than skim what happened finally, but you'll understand. It turned out that Ernie Payton's wife had an extra pair of knickers and she loaned them to Isabelle. I was waiting outside the cabin while she dressed next morning, and she called out to me, 'Oh, George, they fit!' Then I heard her begin to sing. She was a different girl when she came out to go to breakfast. She was almost smiling. She'd done nothing but slink about the day before. Isn't it extraordinary what will seem important to a woman? Gimme a cigarette."

"Fifteen minutes, George," I said as I supplied him.

"Yes, yes, I know. I fished the Cuddiwink that day. Grand stream, grand. I used a Pink Lady—first day on a stream with Isabelle—little touch of sentiment—and it's a darn good fly. I fished it steadily all day. Or did I try a Seth Green about noon? It seems to me I did, now that I recall it. It seems to me that where the Katahdin brook comes in I—"

"It doesn't really matter, does it, George?" I ventured.

"Of course, it matters!" said George decisively. "A man wants to be exact about such things. The precise details of what happens in a day's work on a stream are of real value to yourself and others. Except in the case of a record fish, it isn't important that you took a trout; it's exactly how you took him that's important."

"But the time, George," I protested.

He glanced at the clock, swore softly, mopped his brow—this time with the blue-gray handkerchief—and proceeded.

"Isabelle couldn't get into the stream without waders, so I told her to work along the bank a little behind me. It was pretty thick along there, second growth and vines mostly; but I was putting that Pink Lady on every foot of good water and she kept up with me easily enough. She didn't see me take many trout, though. I'd look for her, after landing one, to see what she thought of the way I'd handled the

fish, and almost invariably she was picking ferns or blueberries, or getting herself untangled from something. Curious things, women. Like
children, when you stop to think of it."

George stared at me unseeingly for a moment.

"And you never heard of Old Faithful?" he asked suddenly. "Evidently not, from what you said a while ago. Well, a lot of people have,
believe me. Men have gone to the Cuddiwink district just to see him.
As I've already told you, he lay beside a ledge in the pool below Horseshoe Falls. Almost nothing else in the pool. He kept it cleaned out.
Worst sort of cannibal, of course—all big trout are. That was the trouble—he wanted something that would stick to his ribs. No flies for
him. Did his feeding at night.

"You could see him dimly if you crawled out on a rock that jutted
above the pool and looked over. He lay in about ten feet of water,
right by his ledge. If he saw you he'd back under the ledge, slowly, like
a submarine going into dock. Think of the biggest thing you've ever
seen, and that's the way Old Faithful looked, just lying there as still as
the ledge. He never seemed to move anything, not even his gills.
When he backed in out of sight he seemed to be drawn under the ledge
by some invisible force.

"Ridgway—R. Campbell Ridgway—you may have read his stuff,
Brethren of the Wild, that sort of thing—claimed to have seen him
move. He told me about it one night. He said he was lying with just
his eyes over the edge of the rock, watching the trout. Said he'd been
there an hour, when down over the falls came a young red squirrel. It
had fallen in above and been carried over. The squirrel was half
drowned, but struck out feebly for shore. Well, so Ridgway said—Old
Faithful came up and took Mister Squirrel into camp. No hurry; just
came drifting up, sort of inhaled the squirrel and sank down to the
ledge again. Never made a ripple, Ridgway said; just business.

"I'm telling you all this because it's necessary that you get an idea
of that trout in your mind. You'll see why in a minute. No one ever
had hold of him. But it was customary, if you fished the Cuddiwink,

to make a few casts over him before you left the stream. Not that you ever expected him to rise. It was just a sort of gesture. Everybody did it.

"Knowing that Isabelle had never seen trout taken before, I made a day of it—naturally. The trail to camp leaves the stream just at the falls. It was pretty late when we got to it. Isabelle had her arms full of—heaven knows what—flowers and grass and ferns and fir branches and colored leaves. She'd lugged the stuff for hours. I remember once that day I was fighting a fourteen-inch fish in swift water and she came to the bank and wanted me to look at a ripe blackberry—I think it was—she'd found. How does that strike you? And listen! I said, 'It's a beauty, darling.' That's what I said—or something like that. . . . Here, don't you pay that check! Bring it here, waiter!"

"Go on, George!" I said. "We haven't time to argue about the check. You'd come to the trail for camp at the falls."

"I told Isabelle to wait at the trail for a few minutes, while I went below the falls and did the customary thing for the edification of Old Faithful. I only intended to make three or four casts with the Number Twelve fly and the hair-fine leader I had on, but in getting down to the pool I hooked the fly in a bush. In trying to loosen it I stumbled over something and fell. I snapped the leader like a thread, and since I had to put on another, I tied on a fairly heavy one as a matter of form.

"I had reached for my box for a regulation fly of some sort when I remembered a fool thing that Billy Roach had given me up on the Beaverkill the season before. It was fully two inches long; I forget what he called it. He said you fished it dry for bass or large trout. He said you worked the tip of your rod and made it wiggle like a dying minnow. I didn't want the contraption, but he'd borrowed some fly oil from me and insisted on my taking it. I'd stuck it in the breast pocket of my fishing jacket and forgotten it until then.

"Well, I felt in the pocket and there it was. I tied it on and went down to the pool. Now let me show you the exact situation." George seized a fork. "This is the pool." The fork traced an oblong figure on the tablecloth. "Here is Old Faithful's ledge." The fork deeply marked this impressive spot. "Here are the falls, with white water running to here. You can only wade to this point here, and then you have an abrupt six-foot depth. 'But you can put a fly from here to here with a long line,' you say. No, you can't. You've forgotten to allow for your back cast. Notice this bend here? That tells the story. You're not more than twenty feet from a lot of birch and what not, when you can no longer wade. 'Well then, it's impossible to put a decent fly on the water above the sunken ledge,' you say. It looks like it, but this is how it's done: right here is a narrow point running to here, where it dwindles off to a single flat rock. If you work out on the point you can jump across to this rock—situated right here—and there you are, with about a thirty-foot cast to the sunken ledge. Deep water all around you, of course, and the rock is slippery; but—there you are. Now notice this small cove, right here. The water from the falls rushes past it in a froth, but in the cove it forms a deep eddy, with the current moving round and round, like this." George made a slow circular motion with the fork. "You know what I mean?"

I nodded.

"I got out on the point and jumped to the rock; got myself balanced, worked out the right amount of line and cast the dingaree Bill had forced on me, just above the sunken ledge. I didn't take the water lightly and I cast again, but I couldn't put it down decently. It would just flop in—too much weight and too many feathers. I suppose I cast it a dozen times, trying to make it settle like a fly. I wasn't thinking of trout—there would be nothing in there except Old Faithful—I was just monkeying with this doodlebug thing, now that I had it on.

"I gave up at last and let it lie out where I had cast it. I was standing there looking at the falls roaring down, not thinking about anything in particular, when I remembered Isabelle, waiting up on the trail. I raised my rod preparatory to reeling in and the what-you-may-call-'em made a kind of a dive and wiggle out there on the surface. I reached for my reel handle. Then I realized that the thingamajig wasn't on the water. I didn't see it disappear, exactly; I was just looking at it, and then it wasn't there. 'That's funny,' I thought, and struck instinctively. Well, I was fast—so it seemed—and no snags in there. I gave it the butt three or four times, but the rod only bowed and nothing budged. I tried to figure it out. I thought perhaps a water-logged timber had come diving over the falls and upended right there. Then I noticed the rod take more of a bend and the line began to move through the water. It moved out slowly, very slowly, into the middle of the pool. It was exactly as though I was hooked onto a freight train just getting under way.

"I knew what I had hold of then, and yet I didn't believe it. I couldn't believe it. I kept thinking it was a dream, I remember. Of course, he could have gone away with everything I had any minute if he'd wanted to, but he didn't. He just kept moving slowly, round and round the pool. I gave him what pressure the tackle would stand, but he never noticed a little thing like that, just kept moving around the pool for hours, it seemed to me. I'd forgotten Isabelle; I admit that. I'd forgotten everything on earth. There didn't seem to be anything else on earth, as a matter of fact, except the falls and the pool and Old Faithful and me. At last Isabelle showed up on the bank above me, still lugging her ferns and what not. She called down to me above the noise of the falls. She asked me how long I expected her to wait alone in the woods, with night coming on.

"I hadn't had the faintest idea how I was going to try to land the fish until then. The water was boiling past the rock I was standing on, and I couldn't jump back to the point without giving him slack and perhaps falling in. I began to look around and figure. Isabelle said, 'What on earth are you doing?' I took off my landing net and tossed it to the bank. I yelled, 'Drop that junk quick and pick up that net!' She said, 'What for, George?' I said, 'Do as I tell you and don't ask questions!' She laid down what she had and picked up the net and I told her to go to the cove and stand ready.

"She said, 'Ready for what?' I said, 'You'll see what presently. Just stand there.' I'll admit I wasn't talking quietly. There was the noise of the falls to begin with, and—well, naturally I wasn't.

"I went to work on the fish again. I began to educate him to lead. I thought if I could lead him into the cove he would swing right past Isabelle and she could net him. It was slow work—a three-ounce rod—imagine! Isabelle called, 'Do you know what time it is?' I told her to keep still and stand where she was. She didn't say anything more after that.

"At last the fish began to come. He wasn't tired—he'd never done any fighting, as a matter of fact—but he'd take a suggestion as to where to go from the rod. I kept swinging him nearer and nearer the cove each time he came around. When I saw he was about ready to come I yelled to Isabelle. I said, 'I'm going to bring him right past you, close to the top. All you have to do is to net him.'

"When the fish came round again I steered him into the cove. Just as he was swinging past Isabelle the stuff she'd been lugging began to roll down the bank. She dropped the landing net on top of the fish and made a dive for those leaves and grasses and things. Fortunately the net handle lodged against the bank, and after she'd put her stuff in a nice safe place she came back and picked up the net again. I never uttered a syllable. I deserve no credit for that. The trout had made a surge and shot out into the pool and I was too busy just then to give her any idea of what I thought.

"I had a harder job getting him to swing in again. He was a little leery of the cove, but at last he came. I steered him toward Isabelle and lifted him all I dared. He came up nicely, clear to the top. I yelled, 'Here he comes! For God's sake, don't miss him!' I put everything on the tackle it would stand and managed to check the fish for an instant right in front of Isabelle.

"And this is what she did: it doesn't seem credible—it doesn't seem humanly possible; but it's a fact that you'll have to take my word for. She lifted the landing net above her head with both hands and brought it down on top of the fish with all her might!"

George ceased speaking. Despite its coating of talcum powder, I was able to detect an additional pallor in his countenance.

"Will I ever forget it as long as I live?" he inquired at last.

"No, George," I said, "but we've just exactly eleven minutes left."

George made a noticeable effort and went on:

"By some miracle the fish stayed on the hook; but I got a faint idea of what would have happened if he'd taken a real notion to fight. He went around that pool so fast it must have made him dizzy. I heard Isabelle say, 'I didn't miss him, George'; and then—well, I didn't lose my temper; you wouldn't call it that exactly. I hardly knew what I said. I'll admit I shouldn't have said it. But I did say it; no doubt of that; no doubt of that whatever."

"What was it you said?" I asked.

George looked at me uneasily.

"Oh, the sort of thing a man would say impulsively—under the circumstances."

"Was it something disparaging about her?" I inquired.

"Oh, no," said George, "nothing about her. I simply intimated—in a somewhat brutal way, I suppose—that she'd better get away from the pool—er—not bother me any more is what I meant to imply."

For the first time since George had chosen me for a confidant I felt a lack of frankness on his part.

"Just what did you say, George?" I insisted.

"Well, it wasn't altogether my words," he evaded. "It was the tone I used, as much as anything. Of course, the circumstances would excuse— Still, I regret it. I admit that. I've told you so plainly."

There was no time in which to press him further.

"Well, what happened then?" I asked.

"Isabelle just disappeared. She went up the bank, of course, but I didn't see her go. Old Faithful was still nervous and I had to keep my eye on the line. He quieted down in a little while and continued to promenade slowly around the pool. I suppose this kept up for half an hour or more. Then I made up my mind that something had to be done. I turned very carefully on the rock, lowered the tip until it was on a line with the fish, turned the rod under my arm until it was point-ing behind me and jumped.

"Of course, I had to give him slack; but I kept my balance on the point by the skin of my teeth, and when I raised the rod he was still on. I worked to the bank, giving out line, and crawled under some bushes and things and got around to the cove at last. Then I started to work again to swing him into the cove, but absolutely nothing doing. I could lead him anywhere except into the cove. He'd had enough of that; I didn't blame him, either.

"To make a long story short, I stayed with him for two hours. For a while it was pretty dark; but there was a good-sized moon that night, and when it rose it shone right down on the pool through a gap in the trees fortunately. My wrist was gone completely, but I managed to keep some pressure on him all the time, and at last he forgot about what had happened to him in the cove. I swung him in and the current brought him past me. He was on his side by now. I don't think he was tired even then—just discouraged. I let him drift over the net, heaved him out on the bank and sank down beside him, absolutely all in. I couldn't have got to my feet on a bet. I just sat there in a sort of daze and looked at Old Faithful, gleaming in the moonlight.

"After a half-hour's rest I was able to get up and go to camp. I planned what I was going to do on the way. There was always a crowd in the main camp living room after dinner. I simply walked into the living room without a word and laid Old Faithful on the center table.

"Well, you can imagine faintly what happened. I never got any din-ner—couldn't have eaten any, as a matter of fact. I didn't even get a chance to take off my waders. By the time I'd told just how I'd done it to one crowd, more would come in and look at Old Faithful; and then stand and look at me for a while; and then make me tell it all over again. At last everybody began to dig up anything they had with a kick in it. Almost every one had a bottle he'd been hoarding. There was Scotch and gin and brandy and rye and a lot of experimental stuff.

Art Bascom got a tin dish pan from the kitchen and put it on the table beside Old Faithful. He said 'Pour your contributions right in here, men.' So each man dumped whatever he had into the dish pan and everybody helped himself.

"It was great, of course. The biggest night of my life, but I hope I'll never be so dog-tired again. I felt as though I'd taken a beating. After they'd weighed Old Faithful—nine pounds, five and a half ounces; and he'd been out of water two hours—I said I had to go to bed, and went.

"Isabelle wasn't in the cabin. I thought, in a hazy way, that she was with some of the women, somewhere. Don't get the idea I was stewed. But I hadn't had anything to eat, and the mixture in that dish pan was plain TNT.

"I fell asleep as soon as I hit the bed; slept like a log till daylight. Then I half woke up, feeling that something terrific had happened. For a minute I didn't know what; then I remembered what it was. I had landed Old Faithful on a three-ounce rod!

"I lay there and went over the whole thing from the beginning, until I came to Isabelle with the landing net. That made me look at where her head should have been on the pillow. It wasn't there. She wasn't in the cabin. I thought perhaps she'd got up early and gone out to look at the lake or the sunrise or something. But I got up in a hurry and dressed.

"Well, I could see no signs of Isabelle about camp I ran into Jean just coming from the head guide's cabin and he said, 'Too bad about your wife's mother.' I said, 'What's that?' He repeated what he'd said, and added, 'She must be an awful sick woman.' Well, I got out of him finally that Isabelle had come straight up from the stream the evening before, taken two guides and started for Buck's Landing. Jean had urged her to wait until morning, naturally; but she'd told him she must get to her mother at once, and took on so, as Jean put it, that he had to let her go.

"I said, 'Let me have Indian Joe, stern, and a good man, bow. Have 'em ready in ten minutes.' I rushed to the kitchen, drank two cups of coffee and started for Buck's Landing. We made the trip down in seven hours, but Isabelle had left with her trunks on the 10:40 train.

"I haven't seen her since. Went to her home once. She wouldn't see me; neither would her mother. Her father advised not forcing things—just waiting. He said he'd do what he could. Well, he's done it—you read the letter. Now you know the whole business. You'll stick, of course, and see me through just the first of it, old man. Of course, you'll do that, won't you? We'd better get down to the train now. Track Nineteen."

George rose from the table. I followed him from the café, across the blue-domed rotunda to a restraining rope stretched before the gloomy entrance to Track Nineteen.

"George," I said, "one thing more: just what did you say to her when she—"

"Oh, I don't know," George began vaguely.

"George," I interrupted, "no more beating about the bush. What did you say?"

I saw his face grow even more haggard, if possible. Then it mottled into a shade resembling the brick on an old colonial mansion.

"I told her—" he began in a low voice.

"Yes?" I encouraged.

"I told her to get the hell out of there."

And now a vision was presented to my mind's eye; a vision of twelve fish plates, each depicting a trout curving up through green waters to an artificial fly. The vision extended on through the years. I saw Mrs. George Baldwin Potter ever gazing upon those rising trout and recalling the name on the card which had accompanied them to her door.

I turned and made rapidly for the main entrance of the Grand Central Station. In doing so I passed the clock above Information and saw that I still had two minutes in which to be conveyed by a taxicab far, far from the entrance to Track Nineteen.

I remember hearing the word "quitter" hurled after me by a hoarse, despairing voice.

FATAL GESTURE

ANYONE WHO HAS READ "A WEDDING GIFT" WOULD GUESS THAT if you turned George Baldwin Potter loose at an auction sale to get an antique chest for his wife, he'd discover some priceless old Spinoza rods. And so it falls out in "Fatal Gesture," with what results in the life of George and Isabelle anyone might imagine.

Especially anyone like me who, as a child in Beaverkill, heard so often how most of the things in our house had been bought at auction in New York. At that time (the early 1930s) the city was a remote place some five hours by car (with an obligatory stop for lunch at the Mitchell Inn in Middletown, N.Y.) or a long, rattling ride on the old Ontario & Western from Livingston Manor (depot right behind the late Charlie Fuhrer's pharmacy) to Weekhawken and over the Hudson by ferry.

The train tracks were torn up after World War II. But the antiques are still there in the house, some of them real, some of them merely attractive copies. And along with them, still, come faint family echoes of struggles that took place over their acquisition. A huge, rich rug my father proudly bought. (It had to be sent back.) Hot debates about the cost and beauty of fake dark rafters. (They were put in.) References to the one bedroom my father actually got to furnish—without antiques, needless to say, and thus, my mother subliminally conveyed, without atmosphere.

"Fatal Gesture" and "Daughter of Delilah" were written ten years after "A Wedding Gift." My parents' marriage, though it officially lasted through both their lifetimes, was effectively over by then. To the extent that "Fatal Gesture" may obliquely mirror the existential details of life, the narrator seems to be making splendid use of all those trying times spent at auction sales, and perhaps taking a satiric shot or two at his wife.

Any big auction house in action is a fascinating spectacle. The details of this one seem spot on to me. But what interested me in recent rereading was being reminded that by all rational analysis George Baldwin Potter does not seem to be, even faintly, based on John E. (Johnnie) Woodruff, as I used to think when I read these stories as a boy. Why, I now wonder. And I have to assume that it was because I took the narrator literally to be my father, and because Woodruff was my father's best friend.

Fly fishermen of a certain age (and then some) no doubt remember Woodruff as the creator of the spent-wing Woodruff fly. And perhaps also as a great consumer of applejack and teller of tall tales. His account of how he hooked an osprey on a backcast, and was dragged over half of Sullivan County by it, could hold a room spellbound for minutes on end. Was this pure Münchausen? Don't think it. At least, if childhood memory serves, a photograph of Woodruff and the very bird linked together by rod and line was once on display in the Flyfishers Club of Brooklyn.

I remember him as a jovial man with a soup-strainer mustache who liked to play with kids and fished with his bald head wrapped in a woman's silk stocking to protect it from the sun. He favored brown-and-white Bivisibles, but possessed swarms of dry flies that he kept sealed up like captive fireflies in glass mason jars of the kind then used for preserved fruit. He had a car—I think it was a fancy Packard—with a thermometer in the radiator cap. He gave me my first axe—a light single-bladed trail job that I used for years.

Except for the fondness for brown-and-white Bi-Visibles and the passion for fly fishing, nothing in George Baldwin Potter suggests Woodruff. Potter is painfully serious. Woodruff was a jokester far more like another of my father's fishing characters, The Diver, who never calls the narrator twice by the same name. But that's another story.

Even more compelling evidence, in "Fatal Gesture" Woodruff is actually given a cameo appearance under his own name as one of *the anglers bidding against George at the auction. Having bid on a seven-and-a-half-foot three-ounce Spinoza, Woodruff rigs it and starts a casting competition with a medallion on a park-sized Persian carpet serving as target.*

In the story these goings-on merely delay the awful moment when George must face Isabelle again.

Some ten years or so ago, it was my painful duty to report certain episodes in connection with the marriage and rather brief honeymoon of George Baldwin Potter, passionate angler, and his bride, the fair Isabelle. From time to time since then, sympathetic readers of the narrative have inquired as to the subsequent relationship of that unfortunate couple.

Such solicitous inquiries have taken, as a rule, the following form: "Did George and Isabelle get together again?" To this question, as the years have passed, I have been able to answer, with increasing satisfaction, in the affirmative.

I have become almost lyrical, I now recall, over the continued felicity of the Potter union. One may judge, therefore, with what misgivings I learned of recent disturbing developments in the domesticity of George and his still-lovely better half.

The indisputable source of my information was George himself. I came upon him skulking—no other word describes it—in the shadows of the deserted club library. Since it was now close to the witching hour of midnight, I looked at him with some astonishment.

"Hello," I said. "What are you doing here?"

He did not return my greeting. Eying me with a sort of furtiveness, I thought, he muttered something unintelligible and attempted to edge from the room in a slinking, unobtrusive manner that suggested burglary or worse.

Now, I had left some excellent pheasant shooting on Long Island and come in to town for the night to attend the début, musically speaking, of a female friend of a female friend. Still simmering with the just wrath which the notes of the incipient songbird had brought to a boil earlier that evening, I seized George roughly by the arm.

"Why are you sliding around here in the dark like a crab?" I demanded. "What's the matter with you, anyway?"

George collapsed into a leather lounge chair with a groan. "Why do I always run into you," he inquired, "at times like these?" He groaned again, but sat erect to favor me with a brooding stare. "You're asking me," he said bitterly. "Now I'm asking you. What are you doing here; why should you be snooping around at all hours when a man just wants to be alone?"

"I'm sorry to have forced my way into your private club," I said. "I'm deeply mortified. I blush at admitting it, but I'm spending the night. If you can believe such a thing, I've taken a room here. I hope you'll forgive my—"

Sarcasm seemed wasted on George.

"So have I," he interrupted, and added with mournful dignity, "This is now my home."

"Your what?"

"I said, 'my home.'"

"Since when?"

"Since day before yesterday. I have left Isabelle."

"Not really, George!"

He nodded.

"For good?"

"Absolutely!"

"Why?"

George rose from the chair and faced me. "Her mother," he said simply. He lit a cigarette with shaking fingers and repeated, "Her mother."

My irritation of a moment before had fled. "Life," I thought, "never changes. The old, old story! It goes back to the head of the family, crouching, club in hand, at the mouth of the cave."

Aloud I said, "But, George, why let an interfering old woman, no matter how obnoxious, destroy your—"

"You're all wrong there," said George. "You're barking up the wrong tree. As a matter of fact, she had ptomaine poisoning."

I simply stared.

George grew uneasy under my eye. "Damn it all," he said, "I suppose I'd better tell you everything! Let's go up to one of our rooms. I have a bottle of Scotch."

"Make it your room," I said.

An elevator bore us aloft. George unlocked a door and snapped on a light. We entered.

There are, no doubt, drearier abiding places on Manhattan Island than its various club bedrooms, but I have not, as yet, been forced to occupy one of them. I was able to take in the furnishings of George's sleeping quarters at a glance. Its general color scheme was a corpselike gray, warmed only by a variegated cataract of neckties wedged between the dresser mirror and its support. On the dresser were two ebony brushes, a comb and one peculiarly significant item. It was Isabelle's picture in a tooled-leather frame. She was smiling.

Gazing at the picture and uplifted by the implication of this face beaming upon George dressing, George undressing, George slumbering through the night, I now assumed a manner indicative of gayety and cheer.

"You old mud turtle," I said, nudging him in the side, "you certainly have a lovely wife."

George dashed me to earth.

"Had," said he, and turned the picture face down upon the dresser.

45

"You take the chair," he commanded; "I'll sit on the bed. But wait a minute—" He went to the telephone. "Do you want soda or ginger ale?"

"Never mind ordering anything for me," I told him. "Plain water will do."

"Suits me too," said George. He reached under the bed, pulled a traveling bag into view and withdrew a bottle from its interior. "Ought to be a couple of glasses here. . . . Oh, yes, they're in the bathroom." Presently he was sitting on the bed staring down into his glass.

I sipped in expectant silence. "Well?" said I, at last.

"It's a brownish-yellow thing with shelves," said George suddenly. "Below are two doors with wooden catches. That's all there is to it. I give you my word, that's all there is to it. Don't think I'm exaggerating. I could make one myself out of two—well, maybe three—dry-goods boxes. What do you think of that?"

"Nothing as yet, George," I told him patiently.

"Well, you will before I get through, and don't you forget it. It's called an Early American cupboard. It was to go in the breakfast room. Two of 'em. She had bought one already. The other was to go at the other end of the room. She had done the room over for 'em—new paper, new paint. Yellow walls with Colonial-white woodwork, she said. Think that over. But that's nothing. You may not believe me, but it's the truth as God is my judge. She was going to have a perfectly good hardwood floor ripped out and wide boards with knots laid in place of it. I had it from her own lips. Wide boards with knots, was what she said.

"I remember asking her, 'Why knots?' To show you I had perfect control over myself, I laughed when I said it. I laughed and said, 'Pretty good, eh, darling—why nots?' Can I take it? I'll say I can.

"She didn't laugh. She didn't explain about the knots. She put her head on one side, then she put it on the other. She said, 'George, can you imagine what the delft plates are going to look like on those warm yellow shelves against the mustard-colored walls?'"

George paused and slowly shook his head. "Well, I suppose life is like that," he said, and paused again to stare unseeingly at the floor.

"But, George," I said, "somehow I'm not getting this straight in my mind. Somehow I don't seem to get anything from what you are saying. Downstairs you told me it was Isabelle's mother. Where does she come in?"

"She'll come in all right. She'll come in plenty. . . . Where was I?"

"Frankly, George, I don't know."

"Well, what was I talking about?"

"I think," said cautiously, "that cupboards had something to do with it."

"Something to do with it! I'll tell the cock-eyed world! They had everything to do with it."

"Well, then," I said, "suppose we start with cupboards. Begin right there."

"But, my God," said George, "I've been all over that once."

"My fault, no doubt, but it isn't altogether clear to me even now. Suppose you get this cupboard business straightened out for me. She had two cupboards—was that it?"

"It was not," said George firmly. "She never had two. She had one. I said so distinctly. I'll say it again. She had exactly one cupboard. One—count 'em—cupboard. C-u-p-b-o-r-d—cupboard. Have you taken that in?"

"You left out the 'a' in cupboard," I said.

"I don't care what I left out, so long as I get it through your thick head that she had one of 'em."

"Don't get excited, George," I said.

George set his glass down on the small table beside the bed and threw his arms despairingly in the air. "I give up," he said. "I give up completely. I've lost my wife. You force yourself into the one home I have left, and when I try to tell you, as a friend—as a friend, mind you—coolly, calmly, clearly, exactly what happened, you sit there drinking my Scotch and tell me I'm excited. I simply give up."

"Don't give up, George," I urged. "I've had a trying day, what with one thing and another. I suppose my mind isn't all it should be. Make allowances for me and go ahead, like a good fellow. First, if you don't mind, just skim over this cupboard business again. Where did she get them—it, I mean."

George eyed me dubiously but went on.

"She got the one cupboard—one, mind you—from old Mrs. Touchard, up in Connecticut. The depression had the old lady on the ropes. She was selling her furniture a piece at a time. She'd part with an old, rickety chair that you couldn't sit in three minutes without dislocating your spine, as though it were her life's blood, and live on the money until it was gone. Then she'd let go of a sort of curlicue bed. Isabelle called 'em—let's see—thread beds? . . . No, that isn't it. . . . Rag beds? . . . No, that's the messy sort of rugs they go crazy over."

"Spool," I suggested.

George looked at me admiringly. "I guess the old bean isn't so dead, after all," he said. "Now, how did you guess that?"

"One of them," I confessed, "severed diplomatic relations between two branches of my family."

"That's it!" said George. "You're beginning to get the idea. Well, listen. Did you ever happen to see a picture I saw once? It was an old buffalo standing in the snow. All around him were wolves, just sitting there waiting for him to topple over. Well, the women Isabelle trains with were like that about old Mrs. Touchard. They just waited. They knew every stick of furniture she had. They'd argue about who was to get what. When the old lady had to sell something, there was a riot.

"I think Isabelle was the leader of the pack. She simply lived at the old lady's. She took her port wine—six bottles, pre-Volstead, I had left—until it was gone. She took her jelly and soup and cold chicken. Once I said, 'Listen, darling; your system's all haywire. Just take her cocktails as an appetizer, and let it go at that.' She said I was heartless and disgusting. That's what you get when you try to help a woman."

George broke off, reached for his glass and drank deeply.

"Well, maybe I was wrong, because Isabelle got the prize package. It was this cupboard I told you about six or seven times. Mrs. Touchard had two of them, exactly alike, and Isabelle got one. The rest of the women would hardly speak to her after she told 'em. She sent it somewhere to have it waxed—I think she said—and started in doing over the breakfast room. She said, 'I'm planning the room for both of them, George; one at each end.' I said, 'How do you know you'll get the other?' She said, 'That's what those silly women are being so absurd about.' Then she told me she'd called a meeting and persuaded the crowd to enter into a ladies' agreement that if any of them got one cupboard, it would be a sort of option on the other. She said, 'You see, they're companion pieces, George; they simply have to go together. They all saw how reasonable and fair my suggestion was at the time.' I said, 'Well, then why are they so snooty about it now?' Isabelle said, 'It's all that Grace Witherbee's doings—the cat.' She wouldn't say anything more for awhile, but at last she told me—well, not told me, exactly; I sort of got it out of her—that Tom Witherbee's wife had found out that Mrs. Touchard had already promised Isabelle one cupboard when Isabelle called the meeting. Can you possibly beat that?"

"What did you say?" I asked.

"Not much," said George. "I didn't get a chance. When I suggested—just suggested, mind you—that the transaction might be—well, a bit shady—she went all to pieces. She said, among other things, that it was simply business. That's what she said—simply business. She said I made her sick. She said I did things at the office like that right along and thought it was clever, but that when my wife showed a little foresight—that's what she called it, 'a little foresight'—I talked like the Sermon on the Mount. Then she went up to her room and locked the door, and when I tried to get in, I heard her weeping. . . . How about another snifter?"

"Not yet," I said. "Go ahead!"

"Well, the unexpected happened. Old Mrs. Touchard died. I asked Isabelle if she thought losing the cupboard killed her, and Isabelle

didn't even smile. Funny thing about women—you may have noticed
it—absolutely no sense of humor. The old lady died without any warning. They simply found her in the morning. Isabelle had to bring back
some pound cake, I think it was, she'd taken up to her. Isabelle said,
'It's such a shame. She adored cake. What on earth am I going to do
now?' I said, 'About what?' She didn't answer. She asked a question
instead. She said, 'What do they do about estates?' Now, I ask you to
try and answer that one. I started in to straighten it out. I said, 'To
begin with, who are they?' Isabelle said, 'They are whoever does whatever they do.' I said, 'Darling, that doesn't even begin to make sense.'
Isabelle said—I'll give you her exact words—she said, 'George, I wonder if there is anyone else like you anywhere? I wish there was—I'd
so love to meet his wife.'" George paused reflectively. "After what's
happened," he said at last, "I keep going over things she's said lately,
in my mind. I've wondered about the remark I've just repeated to you.
What do you think of it?"

"If you don't mind," I said, "I think I'll have that drink you offered
me a minute ago, now."

"Why, sure," said George, reaching for the bottle. . . . "Where was
I?" he wanted to know, when our glasses were filled.

"She'd asked you about estates."

"Right-o! I found out what she was driving at a week or so later.
The executor sent what was left of Mrs. Touchard's furniture to an
auction company here in New York, to be sold under the hammer.
Isabelle found out the day it was to be sold, and that was that. She
put a ring around the date on her desk calendar, and she'd go into the
breakfast room, right while the painters or paperhangers were at work,
and stand by the hour. The day before the sale she got a sales catalogue
from the auction people. She was sitting in the living room that evening, poring over the catalogue, when the telegram came. A maid
brought it to her on a tray." George lapsed into silence. He stared
down into his glass for a moment, then looked up haggardly at me. "I
can see that telegram on the silver tray now," he said. "I can see her

take it and tear it open. Little did I think that—" He broke off, was silent for a moment, then raised his glass. "Here's to life," he said, adding, with the glass at his lips, "and a hell of a mess it is."

I joined him in a toast that left him with a beaded brow and an expression that marked him as one of the doomed.

"Nothing," I offered weakly, "is ever as bad as it seems."

George snorted in derision.

"Oh, is that so?" he said. "Well, listen! The wire was from her father. I've still got it somewhere. It said: 'Your mother ill. Wants you. Come at once.' That's what it said. That's what it said exactly. What do you think of that?"

"I don't know what to think yet," I told him. "Suppose you—"

"Hah!" George burst out. "You don't, eh? Well, you will, I promise you that. Get this: It meant she had to go to New Rochelle that night. It meant she'd have to be there all the next day. All the next day, mind you. Now what do you think?"

"Why, George," I confessed, "I've been to New Rochelle once—I stayed a whole week-end, as a matter of fact. I don't see why she couldn't stand it for—"

"You're right," George broke in. "There is something the matter with your head. Well, try and take this in: The other cupboard was to be sold at auction the next day. Now think this over. Of all the days in the year—in nine years, when you get right down to it—that was the day her mother picked out to have ptomaine poisoning."

I remained speechless.

George rushed on: "While a maid was packing a bag for Isabelle, she told me what I had to do. The cupboard was No. 827 in the catalogue. It would be sold, she said, somewhere around four o'clock next day. But she said not to take a chance. She said something might happen to advance the hour. She said, 'George, the sale starts at two. You be there at one o'clock and simply stay right there until they put it up.' I said, 'Darling, surely you don't expect me to sit there twiddling my thumbs from one o'clock until four?' Isabelle said, 'I didn't know that even you would talk about thumb twiddling. I didn't know any one had ever mentioned it since Thackeray or Dickens. I never asked you to do a single important thing before, and now, when I do, with my own mother dying, for all you know, you bring up thumb twiddling.' Well, of course, that settled it. I told her I'd be there at one o'clock, and she told me to find the cupboard as soon as I got there and then keep my eye right on it until it was put up for sale. How would you like to sit and watch a cupboard for three hours? Now, as man to man, how would you?"

George paused momentarily, but was off again before I was equal to a reply.

"I told her I'd do it. That's exactly what I told her. I want you to notice that in this whole business I never crossed her once. Her wish was my law. That makes what finally happened all the more— But never mind that now. I not only said I'd keep an eye on the cupboard, I also promised I'd top the bid of Grace Witherbee or any of the rest of them, if it took my entire bank balance. And listen; this isn't 1929. I expect even you scribbling fellows know that."

"Yes, George," I said, "we do."

"Well, it only goes to show my attitude. It ought to be clear to you by now that I was for the little woman, lock, stock and barrel, let the tail go with the hide, hook, line and sinker." A spasm swept over George's face like a passing cloud at his last metaphor. "Just imagine," he said, "fishing with a sinker. Imagine plopping such a thing into a stream. And yet, up on the Ausable, one day—" George's expression changed. The anxious look left his face, the rigidity went out of his figure. He settled himself comfortably on the bed. "I'll simply have to tell you this. It's really good. I was fishing the ski-jump pool. I was using a No. 12 fan wing, Royal Coachman—early in the day for it—still that's what I was using, I remember. I'd hooked a small native and was taking him off when I saw what looked like a good fish rise about thirty—well, perhaps, thirty-five—yards above me, close to a rock on the right-hand side of the stream. The native had messed up the fan wing some. I was drying the fly before working up slowly to where I'd seen the rise, when a fellow came out of the bushes just above me, carrying—think this over—a steel rod with a hunk of lead about as big as a—"

"George," I interrupted, "if you get started on that sort of thing, we'll be here all night."

"Eh?" said George, as though returning suddenly from another world. "What did you say?"

I repeated my previous comment.

George sighed.

"All right, all right," he said. "I was only going to relate a— But as you say, perhaps this isn't the time for— Where was I?"

"You'd promised Isabelle to be at the auction rooms by one o'clock."

"Precisely; and, believe it or not, I was there at quarter past. The first thing I did was to locate the cupboard. Naturally, I expected to be knocked dead by it. I had it in my mind's eye as a sort of massive, shiny thing, with carving all over it. I poked around until I came to something with No. 827 pasted on it. I took one look at it and went straight to a young man who seemed to be in charge. I said, 'I'd like to call your attention to a mistake.' He was a pale, thin, unpleasant young man, with light hair and sort of pinkish eyes. He said, 'Really. What sort of a mistake?' I said, 'Oh, nothing very serious. If you'll follow me I'll show you.' I took him over to the thing I'd found and pointed to the number in my catalogue. Isabelle had marked a heavy ring around the number and then underscored 'Early American Cupboard' three times. I said, 'You see?'

"The pale young man looked at the number. His eyebrows went up in a most extraordinary way. You'd hardly believe it—they seemed to go right up into his hair. He said, 'Really, I'm afraid I don't.' I began to get annoyed. I said, 'What kind of a place is this, may I ask?' Then I explained patiently that 827 called for an Early American cupboard. The young man said, 'Quite so,' and stood looking at me with his eyebrows up. I said, 'But damn it all, you've got the number on this thing here.' He said, 'Quite so,' again. Then he ran his hand down the thing I'd found and said, 'Absolutely authentic; about 1780. One of the finest pieces we have ever handled.' He let down his eyebrows and went away. I suppose I stood and took in the Early American cupboard for ten minutes. I've told you what it was like. I tried to figure out why on earth any one would give it house room. I gave up and went and sat in one of the camp chairs that were standing in rows from the front to the back of the place. . . . Cigarette?"

"Thanks," I said, helping myself from his proffered case.

"Drink?"

"Not yet."

George lit a cigarette and inhaled deeply.

"Have you ever," he wanted to know, "been in one of these auction rooms?"

"Not that I remember."

"Well, it's depressing," George told me. "So much old furniture and knickknacks and whatnots all around, and the rows of camp chairs and the kind of pulpit thing up front. There were only a few people there—mostly old men with milkish whiskers and thin old women with lorgnettes—poking about and looking at the things that were going to be sold, and not making a sound. I'll say to you I never wanted a drink more in my life. I'd have given ten bucks for a good, stiff pick-me-up. I'd have given fifty if I'd had a flask with me.

"I got out my pipe and started to fill it, but the pale young man, who had been keeping an eye on me in an annoying manner, came and said, 'Sorry, no smoking.' So I just sat there sucking on the empty pipe.

"And now get ready for the most surprising thing you ever heard. I had begun to look through the catalogue just to keep from rushing out to a speak-easy, and all of a sudden I read: 'Consignment of rods and fishing tackle. Estate of the late Andrew B. Jenks.' That is exactly what I read, no more, no less. Can you believe it?"

"I don't see why not, George," I said. "What's so surprising about that?"

"Plenty," George told me. "In the first place, I would have expected to find fishing tackle at the morgue quicker than where I was. In the second place, I'd never heard of Andrew B. Jenks. I still don't understand that. Not in view of what followed. I remember actually smiling, after my first shock of surprise, at what the rods and tackle of Andrew B. Jenks would be like. Yes, sir, actually smiling." George looked at me and shook his head. "Pride goes before a fall," he said, and helped himself to more Scotch. "I think of that smile," he presently confessed, "with humility and shame; but I've got to admit it. I'm telling you now, I once smiled with contempt at the rods and tackle of Andrew B. Jenks." He drank deeply, placed his glass on the table and again shook his head. "I said I'd tell you everything."

I nodded.

"Well, believe me, I am. I hate to admit what I thought next. I thought: 'After all, I haven't anything else to do. Why not go and look the stuff over?' That was exactly the condescending attitude I took. I'll say that's making a clean breast of it. Of course, you know Spinoza is dead?"

"Why, yes, George, I think I do. He died in sixteen seventy something, wasn't it? At—"

"I suppose you're trying to be funny," George broke in. "I'm not talking about that one—whoever he was. I'm talking about Spinoza the rod maker. He's been dead seven years. Of course, the business has been carried on. A son of the old man is in charge. As a matter of fact, they still put out the best rods on the market, but the rods made by the old man himself have something—well, it's hard to explain. They're just different. You simply know, when you get one in your hand, that you've got hold of the sweetest thing that ever shot a line. Not too whippy, not too stiff, sensitive tip with plenty of backbone in the middle, handle heavy fish for years and years and keep straight as a string. Oh, man, those old Spinozas! I've got nine of 'em—no, ten, now—I'll come to that. I'm simply getting you prepared a little for what happened.

"I went over to where I saw the pale young man and said, 'Where are these so-called fishing rods you're selling here today?' His eyebrows went up again. He said, 'The Jenks consignment is in the rug room at the right. We've been informed that it is a particularly fine collection.' I don't know why this fellow irritated me so. It was his eyebrows as much as anything else, I suppose. At any rate, I smiled coldly and said, 'No doubt.' Then I went into the room he had indicated. It was a big room with piles of rugs everywhere you looked. At one end I saw something that startled me. It was a row of leather rod cases standing against the wall—leather, mind you. They ran from one side of the room clear to the other. But that's nothing. That isn't a starter. I went over and began uncasing those rods. Before I'd looked at a dozen I was shaking like a leaf. Listen. You won't believe it, but listen. Every rod I looked at was a Spinoza—made by the old man himself. Every single rod. I remember I thought I was dreaming. There I was alone in that room with forty or fifty old Spinozas. I simply folded up. I had to go and sit down on a pile of rugs. I have never had such a sensation in my life—never.

"I must have sat on that pile of rugs for five minutes just trying to pull myself together. I had sense enough to look in the catalogue and go down the list of rods. Outside of one or two cheap bait rods, everything there was a Spinoza—everything. Light, medium and heavy trout rods. Light, medium and heavy salmon rods. They ran from fairy weight to heavy tournament. I said: 'Oh, my God!' and sat on the pile of rugs staring at the rod cases, for I don't know how long, not thinking especially, just sitting there, sucking on my empty pipe, in a sort of daze. You can imagine the shape I was in. We can only stand so much. A thing like that simply flattens a man.

"After a while I began to think. It began to dawn on me that I was face to face with the chance of a lifetime. It came to me that now I could do something that really counted for the little woman. Get that—for the little woman. That's how my mind was working. How does that strike you?"

"But what had fishing rods to do with Isabelle?" I asked.

"I'll explain it," said George. "It's simply this: No single human being is perfect. Am I right?"

"George," said I, "you are."

"Well, then, I'm going to tell you that I have a—call it a weakness."

"Not really, George?"

"Absolutely!"

"You astound me!"

"It's a fact, just the same. I admit it. I'm not trying to hide it from you. I come right out with it. The fact is, I keep buying fishing rods. Some men drink; some men gamble. I buy fishing rods, and there you are. It has been a constant source of friction between Isabelle and me. Whenever I buy one, I try to slip into the fishing room quietly, without her knowing it. I do it to spare her feelings, naturally. But she has a sort of sixth sense about a new rod. I defy any man to get one into the house without meeting her in the front hall.

"We've had it out dozens of times. At first she used to say, 'But, George, you have heaven knows how many rods now. Why do you buy another one?' That's a hard one to answer. The fact is, I don't know myself. Sometimes when I get home with a rod, I ask myself the same question. But it's too late then. For some years now she doesn't say anything when I come in with one. She just looks at the rod case and then looks at me, while I go past her to the tackle room. Then she goes upstairs and locks herself in her room and stays for hours. Once I said to her, 'Darling, suppose I was a booze fighter, or a woman chaser?' She said, 'Well, that would be more human than this sneaking in with rods. It's queer. It's like taking drugs. It makes me want to scream!' Hell, isn't it? Or, rather, it was. It's all over now." George sighed deeply, drained his glass and lapsed into silence.

"You started to tell me about planning to do something for Isabelle," I urged, at last.

"Yes," said George, coming out of his reverie, "I decided to end my rod buying once and for all. It was certain the old spooks I'd seen in the auction room wouldn't know a Spinoza from a cane pole. I told myself I could buy every rod there for a few dollars each. I thought it all out. Of course, there would be the expense of enlarging the tackle room; but that wasn't to be thought of when you consider what I was doing to spare Isabelle's feelings for years to come. I told myself I'd like to see some slick sporting-goods salesman sell me another rod. I thought I'd let him put it together and wave it in front of my face and then hand it to me. I thought how I'd take it and test it and say, 'Not bad,' and then hand it back to him and march out of the store and go home to Isabelle and my fifty or sixty old Spinozas."

George broke off and indulged once more in rueful head shaking. "Just a dream," he said. "Just an idle dream.

"Well," he went on, "by the time I got back into the auction room, the sale had started. There were a lot more people there by then, all sitting in the camp chairs. Just the same kind of timid-looking old washouts I'd seen before. I sat down in a chair, still in a sort of trance. But pretty soon I got interested in that auctioneer. I don't think I've ever seen any one who impressed me more, at the time. He knew so much, it was simply appalling. It gave you an inferiority complex just to listen to him. No sort of jimcrack could be put up that he couldn't give you the inside facts about. If a Smyrna rug came up, you'd think he'd spent most of his life in Smyrna. The same for Chinese rugs. He knew the province a rug came from like his own back yard. Same about any old rickety piece of furniture. It might be a hundred years old, but he knew the man who made it by his first name, and the day of the week he turned the thing out. There wasn't a corner of the world or a thing in it that could fool him. He'd take a piece of brass, or glass, or china, and glance at it, and that was enough—just a glance and you'd get the facts as to where it was made, and when, and what it was worth. And that wasn't all. He handled the whole thing like Mussolini. No monkey business; no backing and filling—just biff, bang, snap! I remember, I thought after a while that here was the man to lead us out of the depression. I'm telling you this as a warning. It'll teach you never to judge a man too hastily. You'll find out what this fellow turned out to be presently.

"I was awfully cheered by the prices. The way things were selling was a crime. The auctioneer said so. They were going, he said, for a fraction of their value. Judging by the difference in what he said a thing was worth and what it sold for, I figured I'd get my Spinozas for about fifty cents each, case and all. I remember thinking how strange life is. There I was, practically the owner of half a hundred old Spinozas at an outlay of a few dollars, and I had cursed Isabelle's mother, earlier that morning, for getting me into what I thought was a frightful jam. I made up my mind right there I'd invite the old lady to come and stay several days with us—just as soon as I'd got the tackle room enlarged. That'll show you whether or not my heart was in the right place. Why, I know a lot of men who have apoplexy if they hear their wives' mothers are going to spend the night. I'll bet you do, too. Now, don't you?"

"Well, something like that," I said.

"There you are," said George. "That goes to show you. Of course, I've got to admit one thing. I've got to admit I didn't think of Isabelle's mother, or Isabelle, for that matter, much longer. But I'll ask you, when you hear what happened, whether you think any man could think of women or their vague, impossible notions at such a time? I'm going to ask you, as man to man, and I want a frank reply. . . . Where was I?"

"You were thinking of having Isabelle's mother for a visit."

"Correct. And right there I got a shock. I hadn't noticed any one come in and sit down, but all of a sudden I realized that there was some one next to me with a pipe in his mouth. I turned like a shot, and there was John Woodruff. The spent-wing Woodruff is named after him. It's a good fly at times. Why, one day over on the Broadhead, I simply couldn't raise a fish. I tried a Cahill first, I think it was—nothing doing. Next I tried a spent-wing Lady Beaverkill—nothing doing. Then I tried a Skews Hackle, No. 14, for twenty minutes or so—nothing doing. Next I tried a—"

"George!" I broke in warningly.

"All right, all right," said George. "Where was I?"

"A man named Woodruff had just—"

"I'll say he had. There he sat. No getting away from it. I could feel the sweat break out on my face. Beyond him was a row of old ladies with lorgnettes, and he sat there with his pipe in his mouth just as though he owned the place. I said, 'Listen. They don't let you smoke in here.' He said, 'Am I smoking?' I said, 'You've got a pipe in your mouth.' He said, 'I've got shoes on my feet but I'm not walking. . . . What are you doing in here?' I told him I had dropped in to see if I could pick up something for the little woman. He said, 'Me, too,' and began to read a catalogue. I tried to see what page he was looking at. But he kept the catalogue tilted away from me. I thought to myself, 'Maybe he doesn't know. Better divert him from that damn catalogue.' So I said aloud, 'Did you hear about the twenty-inch rainbow I took on the East Branch of the Delaware this season?'

"Well, he simply grunted. But I went on to tell him how I took the fish. Naturally, I gave him all the details. I told him which pool it was and where the fish was lying. I explained how I had happened to see the trout rise while looking at the stream from the road. I told him what fly I had tied on—a No. 10, brown-and-white, Bi-visible—and I showed him just how I'd made my cast to avoid some hemlock branches. In doing so, of course, I raised my arm and made the proper gesture for a loop cast. Do you know just what a perfect loop cast should be?"

"Why, no, George, but—"

"Look!" said George. "Here's your fish." He laid a hastily gathered Gideon Bible on the bed. "Now, then, here's where your fly should light." He dented in the bedclothes with his thumb. "Please bear in mind that it's the leader, not the fly, that, as a rule arouses suspicion in a trout. That being so, how are we going to place the fly here with the fish here, and not let the leader—"

"George," I interrupted, "I'm going to ask you again to postpone any fishing experiences, any instructions as to the pursuit and capture of fish, to a more suitable hour and place."

George laid the book slowly back on the table from which he had taken it. He rubbed out the dent in the bedclothes. He eyed me silently for a moment and said at last, with a slight shrug of his shoulders, "Well, it takes all kinds of people to make a world."

"True," I agreed. "But after all, isn't that a blessing? What if we were all anglers? Think of the consequences to art, medicine, philosophy, business!"

"Business, hah!" said George bitterly. "Why bring that up? Well, anyway, I'll get on with what I've been telling you. As I said, I'd made the gesture for a loop cast. A moment later the pale young man interrupted me just as I was telling Woodruff what the fish had done after I'd hooked him. It seems I'd bid in something when I'd raised my arm. I told the pale young man there had been a mistake. He told me I had one of the greatest bargains of the sale. I said, 'I don't care how much of a bargain it is, I don't want it.' His eyebrows simply disappeared. He said, 'My dear sir, what do you think would happen to us if people made it a rule to come in here and bid in articles and then repudiate their bids?' Well, that did stump me for a minute, and his damned eyebrows got my goat, I suppose, because I told him I was not in the habit of repudiating anything, and asked him what he claimed I'd bought. He said, 'You have purchased an absolutely brand-new, golden-oak sideboard with heavy beveled mirror, for the ridiculous sum of twenty-six dollars.' I said, 'All right, here's your money,' and gave him my address. He thanked me and that settled that.

"I started in to finish telling Woodruff about the big rainbow, but he had disappeared. I was delighted of course, but suddenly I wondered whether he had really left the place or taken another seat for some reason. I stood up to look around and see if I could locate him, and I got what will probably be the most fearful shock of my life. . . . I'm going to have a snifter before I tell you. Join me?"

"Not just yet, thanks."

George replenished his glass, sampled its contents and lit a cigarette.

"Anyone might have expected what I discovered when I looked around that auction room," he told me through a cloud of smoke. "Any one that hadn't been turned into a plain dope by finding what I had stumbled across that day. You couldn't put up half a hundred kohinoors at auction and keep the business dark, now could you? Well, this was the same thing, only more so. The first thing I noticed was that the last three or four rows of camp chairs were filled with men with pipes in their mouths. Then I saw men with pipes simply massed at the back of the room. And then I got the shock I mentioned. Half the Anglers' Club of New York were there. And that wasn't a starter. There were men from dozens of other clubs—upstate, Jersey, Pennsylvania—I knew most of 'em. There was a lot of the crowd who put up at Keener's and fished the Big River from Roscoe down, and about as many more who stay at Phœnicia and fish the Esopus from the Reservoir up. They stood there not saying a word, not looking at one another—just staring straight ahead—waiting. My heart simply sank into my boots.

"In staring around, I noticed a woman—she was not a bad-looking woman—so my eyes came back to her automatically. I thought vaguely that I'd seen her somewhere before. Then she bowed to me. It was Grace Witherbee. To show you what can happen to a man's mind at a time like that, I remember wondering what she was doing there. That will give you a faint idea of the strain I was under.

"Just then a man sat down in the chair Woodruff had left. He got out a pipe and looked hard at me. Then he said, 'Hail, hail, the gang's all here! My name's Blodgett. Ever fish the Ausable?' I said, 'I have.' He said, 'Ever fish the Margaree in Nova Scotia?' I said, 'I have.' He said, 'Ever fish the Big Sturgeon in Michigan?' I said, 'I have.' He said, 'Ever fish the St. Margarite in Quebec?' I said, 'I have.' He said, 'Ever fish the Gunnison in Colorado?' I said, 'I have.' He said, 'Ever fish the Wahoohoo above Squidjum Lake?' I told him I had not. I told him I had never even heard of it.

"He said, 'Neither have I, brother. I was just putting the acid test on you.' Then he whacked me on the back and asked to see my catalogue. I gave it to him without a word. I had taken an instant dislike to the fellow. As he began to turn the pages he started in to tell me about losing a big salmon up on a Gaspé river. I stood it for some time and then interrupted him. I told him this was not a suitable occasion to listen to fishing exploits. I said my mind was too fully occupied with matters of the moment to profit by anything he might say. He slapped me on the back again, said, 'I get you,' and pointed to the Jenks' rods in the catalogue. Then he looked toward the back of the room and said, 'Boy, we're as safe here as on a trench raid.' I made absolutely no reply of any sort. . . . Your glass has been empty for ten minutes. How about it?"

I hesitated and was lost.

"Make it a short one," I said.

With our glasses filled, George went on:

"I have had some trying experiences in my time," he confessed simply. "But for pure mental torture, nothing has ever equaled the sale that day of my old Spinozas. The auctioneer made a speech when he came to them. It was then I began to realize he was not the man I had taken him for. The speech was little short of pathetic. He said the late Andrew B. Jenks had been a celebrated fisherman—not angler—fisherman. He said the sale of his paraphernalia—think that over—'paraphernalia'—offered other fishers—get that—the chance of a lifetime. Mind you, he used the very phrase that had occurred to me, and I'm no word painter. It was—well, feeble, I felt, from him. Fifty old Spinozas, and I had heard that auctioneer grow really eloquent over cracked dishes and rickety furniture. He wound up by saying, 'I am now about to sell the collection of that celebrated fisherman, the late Andrew B. Jenks. Page 47 in your catalogues.'

"I was sitting there in a short silence that followed. My heart had begun to pound like fury, I remember, when the Blodgett fellow said, 'Ever read his *Brown Trout of the Pyrenees?*' I said, 'Whose, pray?' He

63

said, 'Jenks'.' I told him I had not. Blodgett said, 'Not so hot.' Then he slapped the catalogue and said, 'But Andy had the tools.' My dislike of him was increased by his flippancy at such a time. I said, 'When you are entirely through with my catalogue, I'd appreciate just a glance at it.' He said, 'Sure, brother, I know 'em by heart, anyway. There's a twelve-footer that I'm going to wade through blood after.' I took the catalogue without a word.

"And now get this: The first thing put up was a two-piece, seven-foot, two-ounce dry-fly rod. A man stood on the platform next to the auctioneer's pulpit and waved it in the air in circles—in circles, mind you—and this is what that auctioneer said. He said, 'Now, then, what am I offered for the little fishing pole? Who'll start it at a dollar?' He called a fairy-weight Spinoza a fishing pole. I'm asking you to think that over—and, remember, I'd admired him.

"Well, there was an awful silence for a minute. Then a voice boomed out of the stillness—it was really terrific, everything being so quiet that way, after we'd been listening to the squeaks over doodads and whatnots that had been going on. The voice said, 'Listen, you; twenty-five dollars.' Another voice like a Jersey bull's said, 'That's getting him told. Thirty-five.' Now, that fairy weight had cost fifty dollars new. What do you suppose they took it up to?"

"I haven't an idea, George."

"Well make a guess."

"Oh, forty-five dollars."

"If it didn't sell for seventy-five dollars, may I never step into a trout stream again. And listen; that auctioneer was just a spectator. He never opened his head. He just sat there with his mouth open until he finally said in a weak voice, 'Are you all through? Sold to the tall gentleman in the gray hat on the right.'

"The Blodgett fellow looked at me. I looked at him. He said, 'Get the cripples and children back of the ropes.' I said, 'This is an outrage. It's plain lunacy.' He said, 'If it wasn't for the depression, they'd use poison gas.' I remember feeling more warmly disposed towards him. I suppose it was because we were—well, fellow sufferers, if you get what I mean."

"Yes, George," I said.

"There is no need of going into the rest of it. It was all just as senseless, just as exasperating, as that first performance. One remarkable thing was that as it went on, I felt more and more drawn to Blodgett. After each rod sold for some stupefying figure, he'd never show that he was being cut to the quick. He'd give a sort of dry laugh he had and say something extraordinary. He must have been in the war, because his talk was like that. He'd say, 'Third platoon forward, and don't step on the wounded.' He'd say, 'Into the shell holes, men; it's shrapnel.' Once he said something I didn't understand. I don't think it had anything to do with the war. It was when two men started bidding on a rod after everyone else had stopped. It was a sixteen-foot, wet-fly, salmon rod, and they took it above a hundred dollars. Blodgett said, 'It's better than a natural; it's a grudge scrap.' Now, what would you make of that?"

"I think it has to do with prize fighting," I said.

"I believe you're right," George agreed. "I remember, now, he added something about throwing science to the winds and slugging toe to toe. He was an unusual person. I admit that even though he did turn out to be a stubborn jackass."

"How, George?"

"I'll come to that presently. I want to tell you one thing that happened that threw a little more light on the auctioneer. That first rod knocked him out of his stride, but he came back and took charge of the next sale. It wasn't long till he was handling everything like Mussolini again. He kept calling the rods 'poles,' but he'd start each one at twenty-five or thirty dollars and say that seventy-five dollars was just a fraction of what a rod was worth. Once Blodgett said, 'I'll bet he ate up the third grade. He's hell on fractions.'

"Well, anyway, at last the man on the platform began to wave a steel bait rod about. It cost three or four dollars new. I can't imagine why a man like Jenks should have had such a thing. The auctioneer simply rose up in his pulpit. He said, 'Now, gentlemen, I have the privilege of offering you a steel fishing pole—think of it, gentlemen; a fishing pole of the finest compressed steel. Such a pole should last several lifetimes. What am I offered for the steel fishing pole? To be used and passed on to your grandchildren. Who'll start it at fifty dollars?' I give you my word, that's what he said. You could have heard a pin drop any place in the room. The crowd was simply stunned. The auctioneer said, 'Well, then, forty dollars?' No one said anything, of course. The auctioneer said, 'Thirty-five,' and waited. He said, 'Come, come, gentlemen. Make an offer.' There was another silence, and then a voice said, 'Fifty cents to get it out of the way, and you keep it for your own grandchildren.'"

George broke off and chuckled. "Not bad, if you ask me," he said. "You should have seen that auctioneer. It took all the Mussolini out of him. He said, 'I'm licked. I quit. Make your own prices, gentlemen.'" George chuckled again, then suddenly sobered. "That was the only light moment of the rod sale. All the rest was just a sort of horrible nightmare, as far as I was concerned. You can understand that, after what I'd planned to do for Isabelle."

"Yes, George," I said, "but what about Blodgett disappointing you in the end?"

"Disappointing me!" George exclaimed. "Well, I hope so! I told you he proved to be a stubborn jackass. I'll tell you what happened and you can decide whether I've overstated it or not. You remember I'd looked at a dozen or so rods before the sale. Well, one of 'em had impressed me particularly. I had even noted its number in the catalogue. It was a twelve-foot dry-fly salmon rod that was just simply a poem. It was a two-handed rod—make no mistake about that—two-handed. Of course, there is a school of thought that's trying to foist single-handed dry-fly salmon rods on the anglers of this country, and what do you suppose they advocate? They favor a longer butt that fits into a hollow in the actual butt of the rod after you hook your fish. Of all the cock-eyed notions, that beats them all In the first place, a single-handed rod at the required weight will simply break your wrist in two before you've fished it half a day. In the second place—"

"I know, George," I said, "but what about Blodgett?"

"But you don't know," George informed me heatedly. "You don't know the half of it. You don't know a tenth of it. I haven't even started to tell you. Why, I could keep giving you reasons from now until morning, why single-handed salmon rods, dry or wet, are simply—"

"That's just it, George," I managed to break in. "I couldn't possibly sit here until morning. Get back to your friend Blodgett, like a good fellow."

"Don't call him my friend," said George. "Not after— Listen. I'd been sitting there in a sort of a torture chamber, watching my old Spinozas go, one after another. I'd make an extravagant bid on one now and then, but mere extravagance wouldn't get you a ferrule off one of those rods. If you wanted a rod you had to go hog wild.

"Well, they'd worked so far down the list of rods that I knew something had to be done or I'd walk out without one single old Spinoza to show for all my plans and the hours I'd spent there.

"I decided, finally, that I'd take home the twelve-foot salmon rod that I'd liked particularly, or bust a G string. When it came up, I let it go to forty dollars, and was about to bid when Blodgett, out of a clear sky, said, 'Fifty.' I thought, 'He doesn't know I want this rod,' so I gave him a friendly smile and said, 'Sixty.' He looked at me quickly. He didn't smile back. He said, 'Seventy.'

"I felt my earlier dislike of him begin to return. I gave him a look in which there was no smile, I assure you, and asked him, coldly, a point-blank question. I said, 'Why are you bidding?' He said, 'This is the baby I've been waiting for, major.' I said, 'I'll have to tell you I particularly want this rod.' Then I bid, 'Seventy-five.' Blodgett said, 'Eighty.' I said, 'Are you going to keep on with this?' Blodgett said,

'Report to G.H.Q. that we're holding our position in the face of heavy fire.' I bid eighty-five. Blodgett bid ninety. I bid ninety-five. Blodgett bid a hundred. For a moment I hesitated, I confess it. The rod cost seventy dollars new. Then I thought about Blodgett using, or rather misusing, that old Spinoza—casting short, sloppy casts with it, no doubt. Letting the fly and leader smack down on the water, in all probability. I turned and looked him in the eye and bid one hundred and twenty-five dollars in a loud, clear voice. Blodgett got up from his seat. He called out, 'Stretcher bearers, stretcher bearers!' and went out of the place with every one looking at him. Curious performance, wasn't it? His stubbornness cost me about fifty dollars."

George refreshed himself from his glass and went on.

"When all the rods and a lot of reels, lines, leader boxes, et cetera, had been sold, the gang paid at the cashier's window for what they'd bought and then made a bee line for the rug room to test their rods. I put mine together, tested it for a moment or so, and then started to show it to men I knew. Not a man was interested in my rod. They all, without a single exception, tried to get me to look at theirs. Extraordinary how self-centered most men are. Have you noticed it?"

"Well, yes, I come across it now and then," I confessed.

"I regret what followed," George went on. "I admit it frankly. It had a decided bearing on what finally happened to Isabelle and me. I feel certain that despite the strain I'd been under, I should have remembered the purpose of my visit to the auction rooms shortly after the rod sale was over. As a matter of fact, I did remember eventually. It came to me with startling clearness. I'll get to that presently. The fact remains that my mind was confused, not to say numbed, by all that had happened. You can readily understand that. It was now further distracted in a quite unexpected manner.

"It seemed that Woodruff, whom I had encountered earlier that afternoon, had not left the auction room. He had remained for the sale and had brought a seven-and-a-half-foot, two-piece, three-ounce dry-fly rod. He somehow conceived the idea of rigging the rod with a

Vomber reel and a Gebhart tapered line, Size F, he had secured from the sale of tackle, and after tying on a leader and fly, standing at the edge of one rug and casting for a medallion in the center of another rug.

"Well, the idea took like wildfire. Presently it became a series of casting matches for a stake. Each man put a dollar in the pool. He was then allowed one cast. The best casts were marked on the rug with a piece of chalk. The nearest cast to the exact center of the medallion won the pool. You'd be surprised how absorbing those competitions became. Each pool contained about thirty dollars. Woodruff, I noticed, won most of them. I was not lucky enough to win a pool for some time. I had contributed twenty-two dollars, I remember, before I succeeded in winning. This left me eight dollars to the good. At that precise moment it came to me that I had to go back to the auction room to purchase the cupboard for Isabelle.

"I excused myself, returned to the auction room and was really startled to find that the cupboard had already been put up and sold. The thought occurred to me that if I could find the purchaser I might yet get the cupboard by offering an advance over the price paid.

"I went to the cashier's window and asked for the name of the purchaser. The cashier referred to her slips and told me No. 827 had been sold to Mrs. Thomas H. Witherbee. She started to give me the address, but I told her it wasn't necessary, and asked to use the telephone. I called up the Witherbees', but Grace was out. I went home and called up again, and she had just returned. When she came to the phone, I explained what I wanted and asked her if she would take a very substantial advance over what she had paid, for the cupboard. This is what she said. She said, 'All the money you've got, George Potter, wouldn't buy that cupboard, and please tell Isabelle I said so.' Strange about women. Apaches aren't a marker to 'em.

"Well, I was pretty sick, after Grace tomahawked me that way, but just before dinner a truck drove up with the sideboard I'd bought. I'd forgotten the thing completely. I told them to put it in the breakfast

room and went in to look at it when it was unwrapped. I was worried,
I admit that. Naturally, I didn't want to disappoint Isabelle, even
though I'd done everything humanly possible to get the cupboard for
her. I was worried, as I say, until I got a look at what I'd bought. Then
I cheered up mighty quick. The pale young man hadn't overstated it a
particle. I want to tell you that sideboard looked as though it had just
come from the factory. There wasn't a dent or a scratch on it. It had
a polish you could see your face in. And the brass handles on the
drawers looked as though they'd never been so much as touched. The
beveled mirror was there, just as the pale young man had said, and
it was a corker. Furthermore—and now get this—the sideboard was
yellow—you'll remember how she had gone on about the yellow
shelves. It was just a happy accident, I thought. I was just luckier than
I really deserved to be.

"When you consider what I'd been through that day, I felt pretty
good after dinner. Fact is, I was kind of anxious to have Isabelle get
back and see what I'd bought her for twenty-six dollars, instead of her
dilapidated cupboard. I got out my newest old Spinoza and put it together. I took it into the front hall where I'd have plenty of room to
swing it.

"I was standing there testing the rod, when the front door opened.
It was Isabelle. I hadn't expected her, of course. I thought for a minute
that her sixth sense about rods had brought her all the way from New
Rochelle to arrive just when I had it in the front hall. Well, naturally,
I began to explain at once. I told her it was an old Spinoza. I said,
'Think of it—an old Spinoza, darling. They were selling them at that
place you sent me to. Can you believe it?'

"She never even looked at the rod. She said, 'Oh, George, I've been
perfectly awful. Mother had ptomaine poisoning.' I said, 'Well, darling,
you didn't give it to her, did you?' Isabelle said, 'She's better, but I
shouldn't have left her; I simply couldn't wait. Where is it?' I said,
'Where is what?' She said, 'Where is my cupboard—my Early American
cupboard? Don't tell me it hasn't come yet. I couldn't bear it.' I said,

'Now, I'll explain about that, too, darling. There was a little slip.' I'll give you my word, she went as white as a sheet. She said, 'You didn't get it?' I said, 'I'm afraid I didn't, darling. Grace Witherbee beat me to the cupboard. But don't you worry. Don't you worry for a minute. I got something else.' She stood there just opening and closing her mouth in the queerest way. Then she said, 'George, not Grace Witherbee?' I said, 'Never mind her, darling, you wanted something yellow, didn't you? Well, that's exactly what I got, and not a scratch on it. It's in the breakfast room.'

"She went to the breakfast room without a word. I took the rod down and followed her. When I got to the breakfast room door, she was standing in front of the sideboard staring at it. I give you my word, she didn't look human. Her eyes seemed to be starting from her head. She was saying, 'Oh, God! Oh, God!' over and over again. And now listen carefully. Here is exactly what I said, no more and no less. I won't add or subtract one syllable. I said, 'Don't you like it, darling?' that's what I said. Is there anything in the slightest degree offensive in that question, I ask you?"

I was gripped by emotions too deep for utterance. I could only gaze at George and maintain a frozen silence.

"You needn't answer," said he. "Obviously not. And yet, those simple words unloosed on me such a tirade, such abuse, as I had never dreamed could pass a woman's lips." George ceased abruptly and dropped his head in his hands.

I waited for several moments.

"After all," I offered at last, "mere words aren't to be weighed against ten years of—er—devotion."

George raised his head and looked at me with bloodshot, haggard eyes.

"Mere words!" he said. "Do you know what she called me?"

"No, George, I don't, but—"

"I'll say you don't, and you never will—she was once my wife. But I'll say this much: I don't yet know where she ever learned such words.

I can't yet understand how a girl of breeding—a girl who had led a sheltered life—ever heard such appalling epithets, let alone use them."

"But after all, George," I said, "this is a modern age. Women are no longer helpless, overly nice creatures. You must consider that when—"

George held up his hand to stop me.

"Useless," he said, with quiet dignity. "Absolutely useless. I appreciate your motives, but—" He broke off, regarded me cautiously for a moment, looked around the room as though to assure himself that no possible eavesdropper shared our privacy, then, "Listen," he said hoarsely, "you don't know everything yet."

"Is there more?"

"More? You haven't heard anything. I thought I wouldn't tell you. As I've already said, she was once my wife. Naturally I don't like to blacken her character beyond a certain point. But, after all, facts are facts. We've got to admit that."

"Yes, George, but don't tell me anything you don't care to."

"H-m-m," said George doubtfully. He got up, paced the room nervously for a moment, took a drink and returned to the bed. "I think I'll tell you," he said at last. "I owe it to myself."

"All right," I said. "Go ahead!"

George unconsciously lowered his voice and went on.

"I was standing there simply stupefied by the things she was saying—simply stupefied. She kept it up until she ran out of breath. Then she began to stare at the sideboard again. She seemed to be looking at the mirror. She said, 'It isn't possible! It just isn't possible!' Suddenly, without the slightest warning, she snatched the middle joint of the rod from my hand and crashed it with all her strength into the sideboard mirror. Can you conceive of such a wanton, such a monstrous, act? Now can you?"

George rose and again took to pacing the floor. "Unbelievable!" he muttered, mopping his brow. "And yet I saw it with my own eyes. The middle joint of an old Spinoza!"

"Did it break the mirror?" I asked innocently, after giving him time to control his feelings.

George halted in his stride and whirled upon me.

"The mirror!" he roared. "Do you suppose I looked at the damned mirror? She broke the rod joint in two about three inches below the upper ferrule. Of course that ended our married life." He sank down on the bed and again buried his head in his hands.

"George," I said after a silence, "time works wonders. Just now you feel—"

"Don't talk about time," said George. "Do you think any man could ever forgive such willful, wicked, inhuman destruction? Never mind what she called me. Let that go. Just take the breaking of that middle joint—nothing else. Why, it will be years before I can bring myself to see her again, let alone—"

The telephone bell exploded suddenly within the narrow confines of those four drab walls. George leaped from the bed to the instrument as though galvanized.

"Hello," I heard. "Yes, Isabelle, this is George. . . . Oh, darling, not really! . . . Oh, darling, so am I! . . . Will I? In twenty minutes. Maybe fifteen."

George hung up abruptly, turned and dove under the bed for his bag.

"Lonesome!" he shouted at me. "Lonesome! What do you know about that?"

In not over one minute from the end of that telephone conversation between husband and wife I found myself alone. I had become the sole occupant of the late sleeping quarters of George Baldwin Potter. The neckties, I noticed, were gone. The empty dresser missed those warming bits of color. I recalled seeing the ends of several of them trailing from a closed traveling bag as it was borne, like a hurricane, toward the elevator.

DAUGHTER OF DELILAH

BY AND LARGE THE FISHERMEN *I* KNOW DO NOT LONG FOR THE
*Elysian fields. They long for a house in the country where they can
work, making a living somehow, and beside it a stretch of private
stream they can stroll to from their living rooms to fish the evening
rise. It is Isabelle's shameless exploitation of this universal fantasy
that sets "Daughter of Delilah" going.*

*From the lore of auctions we move to the pitfalls of real estate
and the mechanics of stocking trout. Art imitates life clearly in one
detail—the ordering of big rainbows from a fish hatchery near the
Beaverkill. Just about the last thing I remember my parents doing
together—in the early thirties—was buying five hundred fat yearling
rainbows to stock Clear Lake on which, a few hundred feet from the
house, their land conveniently abutted.*

*For me as a small boy, the best part was that they both cast for
these fish using barbless dry flies, and played them in, one by one,
from the central pool of a small fish hatchery on the Willowemoc
near Debruce. Once caught, the trout were trucked to the lake.
Tests had been made, like those George is forced to resort to in this
story, and the thought was that rainbows just might flourish there.
The lake is small, fifty feet deep near the center, spring fed and ice
cold beneath the surface even in summer. It is filled with leeches
that, it turned out, rainbows like to eat—but, alas, also with sunfish
and grass pickerel.*

*There were other predators. In the early weeks neighbors came at
night with bait rods, horsing out the hatchery-fresh and hungry fish
by the dozen. But for a year Clear Lake was full of rainbows. And
even after they were mostly gone, for years in fact, an unwitting*

fisherman, trolling after pickerel with a big spoon would now and then tie into a great, deep rainbow, wily, pickerel-proof and as long as your arm.

Whether my father got the idea for "Daughter of Delilah" from that experiment, or vice versa, I do not know. It is interesting, though, that Isabelle, in this story thoroughly repentant and in the wrong (she has done wicked things, after all!) is given more speaking lines and is a lot more human.

"We're going into rehearsal Thursday at the Avon. Tryout at Westport. See you at the theater." I heard the click of the receiver at the other end of the wire. It sounded like a metallic trump of doom. In this heat! Why did I insist on writing plays?

Almost immediately the telephone rang again. A female voice, having assured me that Western Union was speaking, continued as follows: "Will meet eight o'clock train Wednesday evening. Bring frog gig."

"What's that?"

The message was repeated.

"I don't get the last word."

"G, like in 'George.' I, like in 'Ida.' G, like in 'George'—gig."

"Oh. And the word before it, please."

"F, like in 'Frank.' R, like in 'Robert.' O, like in 'ocean.' G, like in 'George.'—frog."

"Frog gig—two words—is that it?"

"Yes, sir."

I hung up, stood a moment in thought, then headed for my study and a dictionary.

"Gig," I read, "a light, two-wheeled, one-seated vehicle for one horse." Only one horse! Suppose somebody hitched a pair to it—then what? "A machine for raising nap on cloth by passing it over cylinders armed with teasels." Dear, dear! "A ship's boat in which the oarsmen are seated on alternate thwarts." I hadn't known that alternate seating was essential. "Any whirling toy." Would that include my brain, at the moment? "A frolic. A queer figure; oddity. A fancy, whim, joke." Joke, eh? Ha-ha! "A prolonged fish spear." Now we're getting somewhere. "A set of hooks for catching fish by dragging." H'm'm! No frogs as yet, but sneaking up on them, perhaps. "Gigantesque." What on earth? "Suited to giants." I closed the dictionary and wiped my brow.

Now what? I couldn't spend two weeks in Maine as I had hoped, but at least the frog gig, if there was such a thing between the Battery and Harlem, would prove that I could be depended on in a crisis. I called a taxi and sallied forth in the oven-like temperature of Manhattan Island in mid-July.

Presently I faced a miraculously cool-looking clerk across a counter of the most sumptuous sporting-goods store in the world.

"I want to look at frog gigs," I told him, with feigned assurance.

"Yes, sir," he said briskly. "We have only one type, a three-pronged, tempered-steel gig with six-foot ash handle."

Controlling an impulse to embrace the man, I admitted that the gig described was about what I wanted.

"I'll pay for it," I told him. "I want it sent by parcel post to Maine."

And then, as I waited for my change, I became aware of a solid figure stationed before a counter farther down the aisle. It proved to be George Baldwin Potter, angler extraordinary. He was staring at a display of salmon flies to which his particular section of the showcase was devoted.

I moved to his side and spoke his name.

"Why aren't you in a trout stream?" I asked.

George stiffened where he stood. I was amazed to have him turn and give me a bitter, not to say malevolent look.

"What are you doing in here?" he demanded.

"Buying a frog gig," I told him loftily.

George grunted.

"Messy business. Where you going to gig?"

I hastened to explain.

"And you've got to stay in town three weeks?"

"Beginning Thursday."

"Good God," said George. His expression softened. "We're in—" he hesitated. "Connecticut," he exploded suddenly. "She's wild about it."

There being just one "she" in George's world, he was referring, obviously, to the blonde and blue-eyed Isabelle, wife of his bosom.

"What about you?" I asked, with a suspicion that once again, as in the past, the points of view of this interesting couple had failed to meet.

"Hah!" said George. He returned to the salmon flies, extracted a plum-colored handkerchief from his breast pocket and applied it furiously to the back of his neck.

Something wrong somewhere, no doubt of that. . . . I decided to probe for details.

"What's the matter? Isn't it cool out there?"

"Cool!" George whirled from the showcase, his face an even richer shade of purple than the handkerchief. "It had better be. It cost me a cool hundred thousand."

"That's a lot in these days."

"You're telling me. And listen; you must come out. I want you to see what I got for my money. I want you to see just how far a man will go when he tries to please a woman. After you've seen it, I want to ask you a question. I want to ask you if any woman since Delilah ever—but never mind that now. The point is, will you come out and see for yourself?"

"George," I said, "I will. I will indeed. I'll come this week end."

Two days later I descended from the train at Saybrook and looked over the fleet of varnished station wagons and smartly streamlined motorcars that waited, glistening in the afternoon sun.

Suddenly the modern note was violently dispelled by an extraordinary means of conveyance immediately confronting me. It was a cumbrous, high-wheeled touring car of a date so remote in engineering and design as to suggest that this, its creature, was some prehistoric monster, panting loathsomely in a circle of latter-day headlights round with horror and surprise.

"Stop staring and get in," said someone crisply.

It was Isabelle. She sat erect at the wheel of the monster. She wore a print frock of dim lavender, and a sunbonnet of the same shade.

I swung my bag into the back seat and climbed in beside her.

"Of course," she said surprisingly, "it should have been a gig."

"Gig," I said with a start. "Gig? But I sent that to Maine. I brought you candy."

She put the monster, with an alarming clatter, into locomotion.

"What on earth are you talking about," she wanted to know.

"You said gig—did George tell you?"

"George! George doesn't tell me anything, any more." She sighed faintly. "That's why I met you. I want you to use your influence with George. I want you to—"

"Just a minute before we go into that. Why did you mention a gig?"

"Well, you see, it's twelve miles to the station and it's just got to be a car. This"—she struck the small thick wooden steering wheel, set on its upright post, with the palm of her hand—"is a compromise. It isn't right, of course. It's hideously wrong, as a matter of fact. But what can I do? Twelve miles! It should have been a gig with high yellow wheels and one of those white horses with brown specks—if you know what I mean. To be absolutely right for that adorable house, it should be an ox-cart, but I couldn't possibly— What does one do to oxen? Goad them, isn't it? Or is that elephants?"

"Both," I assured her.

"How disgusting. I wouldn't goad anything; not if Nathan Hale and Martha Washington came out of their graves, hand in hand, and begged me to."

"You haven't been doing it to George, by any chance, have you?"

We swerved precariously, missed a rambling stone wall, below banked daisies, by inches and careened back to the center of the road.

"What has George said?" I heard in a quavering voice.

I swallowed until my Adam's apple or heart or whatever it was that had lunged suddenly upward had resumed its normal station.

"Nothing," I said. "Not a word, but I think he's going to."

"Of course, he's going to. He wants sympathy. Just wait till I show you. And after that, if you don't tell George that he ought to wake up every morning in that lovely old four-poster and look up at the oak beams and over at the maple chest-on-chest and wonder if he isn't in heaven instead of just Old Lyme, Connecticut, I'll—I'll never speak to you—I'll never look at you again."

"Would you mind giving me an idea of what's happened? I gathered from George's manner that—"

"Don't tell me about his manner—you don't have to. I've been standing it for three weeks. I'm just about ready to go down to his nasty old river and jump in. 'The river is mine, darling, and the house is yours.' That's what he said before he found out about—" Isabelle broke off suddenly.

"What did he find out?"

A pair of troubled blue eyes swung my way long enough for us to accomplish another lumbering dive for the roadside.

I grabbed the steering wheel and checked the monster's ponderous abandon.

"Suppose we talk when we get there," I suggested. "Now, if you don't mind, just please drive, or let me."

"I suppose you think you'd do it wonderfully. Well, you wouldn't. It took me weeks to learn. Why, it simply leaps at walls and trees and telephone poles if you so much as wink. But don't worry; I shan't talk any more. I've said all I'm going to. You're George's friend; let him tell you. Let him make it all seem terribly low and underhand, if he wants to. You'll probably agree with him. You're a man."

The rest of the drive was accomplished in silence—that is to say, no word was spoken—but the chattering, grinding roar of the thing that bore us along winding roads and at last through white gateposts, left me slightly deafened as I clambered from its embrace and stood thankfully in a neat, graveled drive that had swept up to a wide, white-railinged porch and a high, brass-knockered door.

The house, despite its sheen of snowy paint, had an unmistakable look of age—great age as we measure such things in a young, impatient land. It was surrounded by an expanse of close-cropped lawn from which bulged, here and there, the gray rocks of New England, suggesting porpoises rolling in a still green sea.

Further to the right, the porpoises became distorted whales. From their convolutions rock flowers of many hues and dainty glazed-green periwinkle bloomed and trailed. Phlox, white, pink, lavender, deep purple, with vivid sprinklings of blue delphiniums, observed from above by flaming hollyhocks, crowded casually along inevitable stone walls. There was a spread of shadow over it all, laid by gently sighing elms that seemed as ancient as the rocks themselves. Off to the left, the land fell away to a line of lesser trees that marched beside a gleam of water.

"Lovely," I said. "Enchanting. Especially after New York."

"Wait!" said Isabelle, with a gurgle of joy and an impulsive clutch at my arm. "Wait till you see inside."

My host, despite the clatter of our arrival, had not as yet appeared.

"Where's George?" I asked.

My hostess sobered instantly.

"Sitting by the river, I suppose." She nodded down the slope. "He goes there to brood."

"Brood," I repeated. "In this perfect spot! It doesn't seem possible!"

"George can do it. Go down and ask him why." For a moment, the lady of the manor stood rigid, a sort of defiance in her pose. Then her shoulders sagged, her head drooped, "Maybe he's right," she said dully, and went, without further word or sign, straight through her high white door.

I wandered down the slope and discovered George slumped on a rustic bench, staring at a sizable amber-colored stream.

"So you're here," was his greeting. "Sit down!"

I did so.

"Did she show you through?"

"Not yet. I haven't been inside. She sent me to you."

"Hmph," said George. "That"—he spat contemptuously into an eddy—"is Eight Mile River. I own two miles of it."

"Nice stretch of water. Any fishing?"

George did not reply. His gaze fixed itself stonily on the surface of the hurrying stream. At last he spoke:

"I'm sorry she didn't show you through. It would make my position clear to you. It would make you understand my feelings when it comes over me that I sold a thousand shares of American Tel. and Tel. and put it into a lot of beams and wide boards and a well sweep with a bucket. That's what I got. No use to deny it—that's what I got. I sold my Tel. and Tel. at a hundred and two. It's now a hundred and thirty odd. Of course, there's some furniture that a cat couldn't sit on with any comfort, and then there's the brass knocker and a tinkly thing called a spinet, and a spinning wheel and a cobbler's bench. They're special items. They're extra special. A hundred thousand smackers and I get a spinning wheel and a cobbler's bench. Think that over."

I did so, patiently, knowing how impossible it is to rush George into a disclosure of pertinent facts.

"Well," he went on, "young David What-Do-You-Call-Him and this Betty Whatever-Her-Name-Is got married. That helps. That helps a lot. It makes everything just perfect. They're living in Saybrook in a simply darling cottage. It has chintz window curtains in it. If you don't believe it, ask Isabelle. Chintz, get it?—whatever that is—and it only cost me—you might as well call it a hundred and thirty thousand—a hundred and thirty-four thousand, to be exact. I could have sold the Tel. and Tel. for that last Friday."

"But, George," I said as he paused, "surely you didn't have to buy anything you didn't want."

"I didn't, hey! I've told you already—I told you in New York—I was trying to please Isabelle. I made that perfectly clear, I hope. Do you think a man's judgment is worth anything when a woman's happiness is involved?"

"Well, perhaps not," I admitted. "What happened?"

"It began last winter," said George. "Early last winter. She mentioned it first at the breakfast table. She said, 'George, we ought to have a Connecticut farm.'

"I swallowed something the wrong way, I remember. When I could speak, I said, 'Why?' That's exactly what I said. 'Why?' No more, no less. Isabelle said, 'Because everybody has one.' I said, 'Who's everybody?' She said, 'Well, F.P.A., for one.' I thought she was talking about something the brain-trusters had rigged up that I'd missed. I said, 'What's F.P.A.?' She said, 'It isn't a what. Do you mean to sit there and tell me you don't know who F.P.A. is?' I told her I most emphatically did not. She said, 'Why, George Potter, he's the one who runs the column in the *Tribune.*' I told her the only column worth reading in the Tribune was Rod and Gun. I asked her what this other one was about. She said, 'Poetry, mostly.' I said, 'What has poetry got to do with farming?' You'll admit that's a natural question. I'll go further and say it's the only question that would occur to any man in his right mind. Well, she got up from the breakfast table. She said, 'George, you're hopeless—quite, quite, hopeless.' Then she left the room.

"Nothing more was said about the farm business until spring. She was poring over *Town and Country, House and Garden* and *The Spur* all winter, but I didn't suspect anything until one night when I got home from the office, she flung her arms around my neck and said, 'George, I've found it.' I said, 'Found what, darling?' She said, 'My farm. I've been driving through Connecticut every day for two weeks, and I found it today. It's better than my dreams. No one could dream of such a place. No one. It's too hopelessly, divinely perfect. I've told the agent you'll come out with me Saturday to look at it. Oh, George!'

"Well, of course, I patted her on the back, and said, we'd see. You have to when she gets like that about anything, no matter what it is. You do it in self-defense. You do it for the sake of peace and quiet at the time. Then, if she doesn't get over it later, you gradually, little by little, work her away from the idea. You can understand that?"

"Perfectly, George."

"Naturally, I had no more idea of buying a farm in Connecticut, or anywhere else, than of becoming a wormer. I have a fishing lodge in the Catskills that's just a stone's throw from the Beaverkill, where we've spent our summers for years. Nice comfortable place with good substantial mission furniture that I bought before we were married. I belong to two trout clubs on the Beaverkill that give me nine miles of private water. The river's open fishing from Roscoe to the East Branch of the Delaware. Big water with nice wading all the way. Room for all the back cast you want anywhere along it. Funny thing, though; ten years ago you never took a trout below fourteen inches. For the past few years they've been running from eight inches to twelve. Plenty of food in the river and yet the fish are smaller. Smiley, from over on the Neversink—he wrote *Trout Secrets*, you'll remember—says, 'Too many rods.' He claims that—"

"I know, George," I interrupted. "But let's get this other matter cleared up first."

"Oh, right you are! I only thought you'd be interested in— Well, never mind. Time to talk about trout later; but, boy, don't think there isn't plenty about trout in what I'm going to tell you. You'll be surprised—you'll be speechless, stunned, flabbergasted. You won't believe me—no one could—but I've got the proof right here with me. Right in my pocket. I look at it now and then to assure myself that it really happened. I look at it to convince myself that a wife of mine— But wait, where was I?"

"You were patting Isabelle when she told you she'd found a place she wanted."

"Exactly. That was my attitude all along. I've never spoken a harsh word to her in eleven years of marriage. What other man that you know can say that? Name me one."

"I don't think I can, George."

"I know you can't. And that makes what she did all the more incomprehensible. All the more—well—"

"George," I said, "you're slaying me. For God's sake, get on with it! What did she do?"

"Listen, I'm trying to tell you of a most involved affair. I'm trying to do it fairly, without prejudice, so that you can get a real idea of just what occurred, and you keep shouting at me to 'go ahead' and 'get on with it,' and what not. It's confusing and not especially courteous. Supposing you had been crushed and shattered by one you loved and trusted, do you think I'd keep fidgeting and yelling while you were trying to make me comprehend?"

"Forgive me, George," I said. "Tell me in your own way."

"Very good. Now, where was I?"

"You're still patting Isabelle."

"Yes, of course. I hoped that by Saturday she'd have become interested in something else—Scotch terriers, Siamese cats, blue grass, pewter mugs, copper kettles, Simms' bidding, a new diet or something. But nothing doing. She told me about her great discovery all the rest of the week. It was called High Knoll Farm, she said. It had been a farm first; then the home had been turned into an inn for a number of years; then one of the descendants of the original owners had bought it and restored and lived in it, and was now dead. She said, 'George, get ready to have your heart simply turn over. It's two hundred years old and completely furnished, and there isn't one thing in it that doesn't belong right where it is.' I said, 'If it's that old, it's probably ready to fall down.' Isabelle said, 'Fall down. You should see the beams and the lintels—I think that's what he called them—lintels.' I said, 'Who's he?' Isabelle said, 'The agent. His name is David, and listen, George, he's simply a darling, with wavy hair and gray eyes. And let me tell you something I discovered—he confided it to me in the sweetest way—he's engaged to a girl named Betty Something, and when you buy the farm they can be married.'

"Well, I wanted to say that David was going to die a bachelor, if he waited for me to buy a farm. I didn't say it though. She wasn't in the mood for that sort of thing. I only said, 'We'll see,' again and let it go at that. . . . Would you like to go up to the house for something long and wet, or shall I go on?"

"Go right ahead, George," I said firmly. "Never mind anything else."

George lit a cigarette, his eyes on the stream.

"Look at that caddis fly," he exclaimed suddenly, "just floating into the slick above the middle rock. Watch it."

I followed his eyes to the floating insect. There was a disturbance in the water a moment later, and the fly was gone.

"A trout!" I exclaimed.

George spat once more with due deliberation into the river's face.

"Like hell; that was a chub."

"How do you know?"

"Hah!" said George. "Where was I?"

"It was about somebody getting married if—"

"Sure, and that should have prepared me for the shock I got later. Real-estate commissions are something like 10 per cent. I might have known nobody would plan marriage on a hundred or so. Of course, I'd heard of abandoned New England farms. If you're idiot enough to want one, you're supposed to pick it up for back taxes. With that thought in mind, I went out with her to look this one over on Saturday. The trout season hadn't started yet, and I couldn't duck it and live in the same house with her—not in the state she was in. Why, I even thought, if worst came to worst, I might pay the back taxes and put the deed in her name and let her fuss around with a few old apple trees and some blackberry vines until she got fed up. That shows you my heart was in the right place. That shows you I'm no piker when it comes to my wife.

"We came out on the train—it was quicker, I figured. I thought I'd spend just forty-five minutes out here and catch the 2:20 from Saybrook back to town. This David fellow met us at the station in a car. He was a nice-enough chap as real-estaters go—sort of a moving-picture type. I kidded him a little as we were driving out here, and he laughed heartily at everything humorous I said. Isabelle didn't say a word; she just sat in the back seat, sort of stiff and white. Finally I thought I'd get down to cases. I said, 'Well, young man, what's the bad news? How big a dent do you and my wife plan to put in my bank account?' The David fellow laughed—I'll give you my word he laughed. He said, 'Not so much, Mr. Potter. I can get the place for you for a hundred and ten thousand on a mortgage or a hundred thousand cash.' Well, I'll let you imagine what that did to me. If he'd hit me with a tire tool he couldn't have jolted me worse. Isabelle said, 'That's with the furniture, George.' I managed to turn around and give her one look. She said, 'Now, don't say a word till you see it.' She needn't have worried about that. I couldn't have opened my mouth on a bet.

"We got here finally and went through the house. I've given you an idea what it's like and you'll see for yourself later. The beds aren't so bad. They're about five feet off the floor, with a silly tent thing—a canopy Isabelle calls it—over each of 'em. Comfortable enough, though, after you get into one; but if you can find a single chair that you can sit on for ten minutes at a stretch, I'll swallow it sideways. 'Well,' you say, 'I'll sit on a couch.' No, you won't. There aren't any couches. Just benches without even backs. Just plain pine benches, all nicked and scratched, that have to be waxed for some reason. Every stick of furniture in the house is of yellow wood like the benches, and has to be waxed. The ceilings never were finished. They were just left with the hacked beams showing and, by God, they have to be waxed too. How does that strike you?"

I thought it best to remain silent.

"I got out of the house as soon as I could. My collar seemed to be choking me—maybe you've had the feeling—and I wanted to get in the fresh air. As I stood in front of the house just absolutely quivering with the hellishness of the whole thing, I happened to see the stream down here. Well, you know how water attracts any man, I don't care what condition he's in. First thing I knew, I was standing right here where we are now. I saw it was a nice brook with just about the right flow and plenty of hides, but from the character of the country, I felt sure the water would go close to eighty in the summer, and, of course, trout couldn't live in that.

"Pretty soon Isabelle and the David fellow came down and joined me. He said, 'The five hundred acres that go with the place, Mr. Potter, include about two miles, more or less, of this river. You could throw a dam across at a suitable point and have a splendid swimming pool.' I told him I wouldn't be interested in a stream for any such reason. I told him water had to have trout in it to get any attention from me. The David fellow said he was sorry, but he'd never heard of trout in the river—just eels and chubs, he said. Then he said, 'Are you fond of trout fishing, Mr. Potter?' I said, 'Fond! Young man, the taking of trout on fine tackle with a dry fly is the acme of sportsmanship. I'll go further and say that it's an exquisite art worthy of the best endeavors of any man who lives.' I went on from there and did a little something toward enlightening that young ass about fly casting for trout. I spoke at some length. He stood and listened to me. So did Isabelle. That is, she sat down on this bench, the moment I started, and folded her hands in her lap. When I'd finished, even that real-estater was impressed. I could see that. He said that it had been very interesting. He said he wished there were trout in the stream, so that I could invite him out to learn the finer points some day. That's what he said, 'The finer points some day!'

"Well, I couldn't take that from anybody, let alone a long-legged real-estater that was trying to hand me a pile of junk and a chub stream for a hundred thousand dollars. I said, 'Listen, young man; there are two things that make your suggestion impossible. In the first place, I never expect to own any part of this river, and in the second place, I doubt if you could learn the finer points of trout fishing in twenty years.'

"Going back in the train, Isabelle and I had it out. She said at my time of life I should lend a helping hand to young people instead of insulting them. She said I had blighted David's hopes and probably broken Betty Something-or-Other's heart. She said that she wished she was dead and buried. She said that the only comforting thing about it all was that she soon would be, because I was killing her. She was pretty wild, even for her, but of course I couldn't let her entertain her present insane project for a minute. I told her so. I told her never to mention the subject to me again. She said she would never mention any subject to me again, and she didn't speak to me for more than a week.

"I only got glimpses of her now and then. When I came home, she'd trail upstairs like Lady Macbeth and go to her room and lock the door. Then one morning I heard her singing in her bath, and she came down to breakfast and said, 'Good morning, George,' and kissed me on the top of the head. I thought the farm business was over. That's what I thought. My God, if I'd only known."

George broke off. He clenched his hands in silent agony for a moment; then groaned aloud. "If I'd only known," he repeated, and took his troubled gaze from the hurrying river long enough to give me a wild, a despairing glance.

"Known what, George?" I ventured.

"We'll come to that soon enough. I had a warning at that very moment—if I'd had sense enough to realize it. After she'd kissed me and sat down at her end of the table, I said, 'Well, darling, is it my own sweet reasonable little wife again?' She had begun to pour the coffee. She put the coffeepot down and gave me the strangest look; it actually made me feel creepy. She said, 'I'm being reasonable, George. I feel sure of that.' I remember thinking, 'What's up?' Just a sort of flash, if you know what I mean; but butter wouldn't have melted in her mouth for the next few days, and I forgot it. Then one Friday she went haywire again. The trout season had opened and I was going over into Pennsylvania and fish the Broadhead next day. I told Isabelle. She said, 'Have I been good lately, George?' I said, 'You've been an angel.' Isabelle said, 'Well, then, will you do one little thing for me?' Before I thought, I said, 'Anything, darling.' Isabelle said, 'I want to go to Old Lyme just once more and say good-by to that heavenly place. Will you give up your fishing Saturday and take me? We'll have a picnic lunch out there.'

"Well, she had me. She had me cold. I did some quick thinking and saw a way out. I told her that fishing was against the law in Pennsylvania on Sunday. I told her I'd drive back Saturday night and take her out to Connecticut the next day. She said that would be all right, and helped me pack my fishing stuff that night for the first time in her life. Naturally, I was touched. She'd never been—well, enthusiastic about fishing. It's a sort of blind spot in her. Some women have it, judging by what other men tell me.

"I had a rotten day on the Broadhead. I'll bet I tried fifty flies—kept changing all day long. I had just one rise—a good fish, but he came short. I had been fishing a whirling dun, No. 14, for some time, and I took it off and tied on a brown-and-white spider. There was a nice run, well in toward the bank, and I laid the spider just above a—"

"George!" I said warningly.

"Heh?" said George, with a start. "All right, all right. I must say, though, you're one of the most unsympathetic listeners I ever talked to. You don't seem to care for any of the really interesting details. You just want bare facts. . . . Where was I?"

"You were going to bring Isabelle out here for a last—"

"Yes, and I did it. We came out by motor. Isabelle insisted on an early start. When we got here, she surprised me. She said, 'George, look in the trunk.' I said, 'What for?' She said, 'Never mind what for; just look.' I went to the back of the car and opened the trunk. What do you think she'd packed in it?"

I gave it up.

"A rod, waders, wading shoes, fishing jacket, reel, fly box, fly oil, scissors, net—she hadn't missed a thing. I took everything out and laid it on the grass, to be sure it was all there. Then I said, 'What's the idea, sweetheart?' She said, 'George, I want to sit here, under these great elms, and look at the house for hours and hours. You'd be frightfully bored. I put the things in so you could fool around down in the river and not just sit.' I was touched. There's no getting away from it—I was touched. I didn't tell her that catching chub, when the boys were probably killing 'em up on the Ausable or the Beaverkill, was just a horrible mockery. I said, 'That's awfully thoughtful of you, darling. I appreciate it.' I got into my waders and came down to the stream.

"Well, I put the rod together and tied on something or other and laid it out on that pool you see just below at the bend. I hadn't made three casts when something rose and took it. I tightened and a good rainbow shot out of the water and then went downstream with me. I followed and played him to a standstill and netted him by that leaning tree. I was absolutely bowled over. I creeled the fish—he was a good fourteen inches—and just stood in the stream for a minute, pulling myself together. Then I began to figure it out. I came to the conclusion that the stream must be colder in summer, for some reason, than I had guessed. Evidently there were a few trout in it and I had happened to put a fly over a good one. Finally I began to cast again, still thinking of the sort of miracle that had happened. Well, something smashed at the fly and I struck. This one took me clear down below the bend. He didn't jump, but from the feel of him, I knew it was a good fish. I never got a look at him. He got the leader around a rock, finally, and broke me. I was sweating by this time, and no mistake. I kept wondering if it was a dream.

"To make a long story short, I hooked four rainbows and landed three in less than an hour. The first one was the smallest. The other two were sixteen and a half and eighteen inches respectively. The one that broke me must have been bigger yet. I'll bet he'd have gone over twenty.

"You can imagine, faintly, how I felt. I'm ready to admit that it was close to the top in all my fishing. It was like being struck by lightning—as sudden, as unexpected as that. I figured that there just didn't happen to be any anglers in this section and I had stumbled on one of those virgin streams you're always reading about, right in the heart of Connecticut. I got to shaking so I had to go and sit down. I'd worked up to that round rock there, and I sat down on it and thought. Big rainbow trout a few hours from New York! I began to realize what a grand little woman I had for a wife. I looked up the slope, and there was Isabelle sitting on the lawn looking longingly at the house. By jingo, it got me. There she sat, so quietly, taking her last look at something she'd set her heart on that I had denied her. Right there I came to a decision. I opened my creel. Two of the fish were still alive. I slid them back into the stream—I didn't want to kill too many of my own trout, so to speak. Then I went up and told Isabelle I was going to buy the place. Now you have it. One hundred thousand dollars laid out in cold cash just to make a woman happy. I think you'll admit that's fairly handsome."

I found it best to be occupied in the lighting of a cigarette until George went on.

"We moved out here two weeks later. I was absorbed in the stream from the first. I came to the conclusion that hidden springs kept it cool during the mid-summer, and I spent a lot of time taking the temperature of the water at various places, to see if I could find where they came in. With that and my fishing, I didn't see much of Isabelle, naturally. When I did see her, she puzzled me vaguely, I remember. She was like a wild thing. If I came on her unexpectedly in the house or fussing with the flowers, she'd give a scream and look as if I'd frightened her. I'd hear her singing like a bird, and then suddenly the song would stop as though a thought had choked her. She was mad about the place, of course. She took to wearing clothes that reminded me of tin-types of my grandmother and she bought that God-awful thing she met you in today and insisted on driving it.

"One day, she said, 'George, do you really love me?' I told her not to be silly. She said, 'But what if something perfectly ghastly came between us.' That got my attention. I said, 'What do you mean—another man?' Isabelle said, 'Good heavens, no. I mean, what if I—if you—what if you found out you didn't really know me at all.' I laughed, I remember, I laughed. I said, 'Well, well, well, after eleven years, that would be interesting.' She said, 'I wonder,' and went out of the room.

"I had thought of giving up the Beaverkill trout clubs. What was the use of driving way up there after ten-inch brown trout when I could take all the big rainbows I wanted right on my own place. I mentioned it to Isabelle, but she said not to do it. She said, 'George, you know, after a while you'll get tired of just showing your fish to me. You'll want to talk about three-ounce rods and four-X leaders and things like that to someone who understands what you're talking about.' Well, I saw her point, but when I told her one day that I was going in to New York to lecture before the Anglers' Club that night, she behaved in a most unaccountable manner. She said, 'What are you going to lecture about?' I told her the title of my address would be The Little-Known Connecticut Rainbow. She said, 'Oh, goodness!' Just like that. 'Oh, goodness!' Then she said, 'Please don't go, George,' I said, 'Why, not, pray?' She said, 'I think it's silly, if you ask me. Downright silly.' I said, 'I'm not asking you. I'm not asking you anything. If that's your idea of your husband's ability to make a few remarks about a discovery of interest to all anglers east of the Alleghenies, you're welcome to your opinion.' She said, 'All right, I've done my best.' Then she burst into tears. I left without another word and drove to the train in a thoroughly exasperated mood."

George broke off and slumped down even further into his seat. He remained silent for a moment, staring, as always, into the stream.

"You're great for wanting facts!" he burst out suddenly. "Well, you're going to get 'em. We're coming to the main facts right now, and if they don't simply stop your clock, I don't know what will. I began to notice a disturbing thing when we'd been here about a month. The trout were losing flesh. They kept on losing it until they were mostly heads, with long, snaky bodies. I was worried. I was worried sick. At last I thought I'd get a real authority on the job, and I sent for Bigbee, of Cornell. Isabelle said sending for him was ridiculous. That's what she said, 'ridiculous,' with every trout in the stream just fading away. Well, Bigbee came. He set up a laboratory out in the garage, as soon as he arrived, with microscopes and slides and test tubes, and what not. He said he might have to make an investigation of the food content of the stream. He said, 'You may have a case of too many fish, Potter.' I said, 'But they were fat as butter three weeks ago.' He said, 'Well, feeding conditions change sometimes.' Then he went on to say that he didn't know why four-year-old rainbows were in a stream less than thirty miles from the Sound. I told him I had caught big rainbow all through the Smoky Mountain district that had a clear run to the sea. He said, 'No, they haven't. All those streams empty into the Tennessee River, and that's polluted. They turn back when they reach it.' I said, 'Well, this empties into the Connecticut River. Maybe that's polluted.' He said that might be the explanation. He said he'd take a sample of the Connecticut later, after he'd examined some of the fish. He said, 'Now suppose we go down and catch a few of these rainbows and let me have a look at them.' Isabelle was sort of hanging around listening to Bigbee. She seemed to be taken with him from the first. She said, 'The fish can wait, professor. You promised to let me show you through the house, and I'm going to do it now.' Bigbee said, 'Why, certainly,' and went off with Isabelle, and I came down here and caught some trout for him. When I got up to the house, the car was at the door and Bigbee and Isabelle were in it. His bags were on the back seat. He said he was sorry, but he'd been called away. I was dumbfounded. I urged him to stay. I told him the situation was critical. I told him I was at my wits' end. He said, 'I realize that, Potter, but a very delicate matter calls me elsewhere.' Isabelle said, 'Sometime I want Professor Bigbee to come for just a visit. I think he's a perfect dear.' Then they drove off to the train.

"Well, I didn't worry much longer about the condition of the fish, because a warm spell came along, and just like that"—George snapped his fingers—"there weren't any fish to worry about. They disappeared. I worked the stream carefully for three days and never took a trout or saw a trout—just chubs and a few sunfish. I went down to where the stream empties into the Connecticut River. Just at the mouth I saw some rainbows. They were already in tidewater—the few that I saw. It was a cinch the rest of 'em were out in the Connecticut on their way to the Sound. Well, it was a puzzler—you can imagine. If pollution had held the fish in Eight Mile River until now, what had happened? Had the Connecticut been purified in some way? I couldn't figure it out. I told Isabelle the trout had all gone to the ocean. She got as pale as a sheet. I wouldn't have believed fish could have made that much difference to her. She said, 'Why, it's outrageous, George; simply outrageous.' I thought that was a funny way to put it, but whatever it was, it wasn't any joke. It had me staying awake nights. Tel. and Tel. was up to a hundred and twenty and the market was strong.

"I didn't have time to think about that much, though, because Isabelle began to go really queer from then on. She got sort of furtive, if you know what I mean. She got to slinking around the house, muttering to herself. I began to worry about her. I began to watch her in a quiet sort of way. She didn't seem to want to be with me though. If I came into a room where she was, she'd give me a wild look and then begin to get restless, and pretty soon she'd get up and go somewhere else. We get our mail R.F.D., down at the corner. She always contrived to get it herself. If I offered to go, she'd find some excuse to keep me here while she went. Sometimes, after the mail came, she'd go to her room and I'd hear her pacing the floor. Now and then, I found her weeping. I tried to find out what was wrong. I said, 'Darling, are you disappointed in all this, now that you've got it?' She said, 'Oh, George, I love it. I love it so.' I said, 'Well, you don't act like it. What's the matter?' She said, 'Nothing, nothing, and don't look at me like that. You're always looking at me. Stop it. You're driving me mad.'

"That sort of thing went on for two months. She was getting worse, if anything, instead of better. I thought of taking her in to New York to one of these psychiatrist fellows and let him have a go at her. Before I quite made up my mind to do it, I found her sitting on the steps of the side porch, one afternoon, crying frightfully. It was just short of pure hysteria. I said, 'What is it, darling? Tell me. You simply must tell me.' She said, 'Oh, George, I'm going to be sued and put in jail. Don't let them do it to me, George.' I thought, 'My God! Complete mental collapse!' Then I saw a letter in her lap. I started to take it from her, and she said, 'Don't look at it, George. Please don't look at it!' I said, 'It's all right, darling. Everything's all right.' Then I read the letter. It was from a New York attorney, demanding payment of a statement that he inclosed, and threatening suit. Here's the statement. I told you I had it with me. Just look it over if you will."

George took a folded paper from his pocket, opened it and handed it to me. It was a statement from Cold Springs Trout Hatchery, Inc., Willowemoc, New York, covering the account of Mrs. George B. Potter, 93 East 64th Street, New York City. Its items were as follows:

1000 fourteen to twenty-two inch rainbow trout	$1,000.00
Trucking and planting same	80.00
Total	$1,080.00

I lifted my eyes from the statement and met George's thunderous glare.

"Well," he asked hoarsely, "is that the last word in female duplicity, or is it not?"

But, as is frequently the case when George demands an answer to a question, I found myself unequal to a reply.

THE LOCH NESS MONSTER

THINKING ABOUT INCLUDING MY OWN STORY IN THIS BOOK OF MY father's writing put me in mind of some lines by E.E. Cummings, who once savaged poet and anthologist Louis Untermeyer as follows:

mr u will not be missed
who as an anthologist
sold the many on the few
not excluding mr u

The specific target of Cummings' lowercase ire *was* Modern American Poetry, *a vast collection of verse that, along with works of the first rank, was cluttered by myriads of offerings by minor versifiers, including Untermeyer, who was very minor indeed.*

Though I've published a story or two, I am by trade occasionally a critic, often a book reviewer, and perennially a magazine editor, and I have no trouble understanding that "The Loch Ness Monster" *is no more a match for my father's stories than a sparrow is a match for a sparrowhawk.*

I venture to include it, however, because it is an old-fashioned fishing story that deals, obliquely at least, with George Baldwin Potter. And more directly it takes up some of the matters discussed in these prefaces—the way story-telling makes use of real life: the way a literary character that you have taken to heart for years can seem more alive to you than people you see at the office or on the commuter train.

In its own sneaky, fictional way, for me this story also lays to

*rest a nagging, lifelong awareness of the peculiar expectations and
cross purposes that having a celebrated father (even in the smallish
world of readers who love fly fishing) may exert upon a son. Yes,
there was a George Baldwin Potter. And in a sense the following
story proves it.*

My telephone rang. The receptionist downstairs
said, "A Mr. Potter to see you, sir." On the
other end of the line I heard a man's muffled
voice. "Let me speak to him." Then, after a
click, it boomed in my ear.

"This is George Potter," it said. "We've never met but you know
who I am. George Baldwin Potter III." It paused expectantly.

"I'm awfully sorry," I said. "Are you sure you're looking for me?"

"My father was a madman for fishing," said the voice. "Your father
wrote about him."

"My God," I broke in. "That idiot character who could think of
nothing but brown trout and Spinoza rods. You mean he was real?"

"Of course he was real," said Potter stiffly. "That's why I need your
help." Hastily I agreed to meet him for lunch.

As I walked from my office toward George Baldwin Potter's club—a
large, unlovable place, like an apartment building, just across from
Grand Central—I was still astounded. It was as if Captain Ahab had
stumped into my office, or the receptionist had announced, "There's a
Mr. Butler to see you. A Mr. Rhett Butler." George Baldwin Potter
had no such place as those two in the world of story-telling. But he
was my father's most successful character and, I always assumed, as pure

a creation of fiction as there can be. I remembered him as a maniacal middle-aged party who nattered on interminably about the dry fly on fast water, and kept getting into marital scrapes with his young, non-fishing bride. But even allowing for the embroidering on reality that any story-teller permits himself, it was hard to believe George Baldwin Potter had ever existed. Let alone imagine that he could find the time between domestic spats and monologues on the correct presentation of the dry fly to have a son.

We met at the bar. George Baldwin Potter's hands were the size of hockey gloves. As he turned to the bartender to order me a drink, heavy muscle rippled at his shoulders and at the back of his neck.

"Thanks for coming," he muttered into his drink, barely catching my eye. "I didn't make much sense on the phone." We drank and exchanged information. I learned that he had been an athlete in college—he mentioned track particularly and I remember a fleeting puzzlement. I couldn't imagine so big a man running or jumping, yet I had a feeling I'd heard of him during my own college days.

Now he worked downtown in an investment house. He was single—but hoped not to be for long. Awkward silence. Then, after a glum examination of his double martini he mumbled, "Let's go in and have some oysters."

We did. He ate his twelve in fast gulps, wiped his mouth and drew a breath. "The truth is," George Baldwin Potter said with an uneasy glance to either side of us, "I have to ask you a tremendous favor."

Since he clearly wasn't going to ask for money, I pronged another oyster and nodded encouragingly.

"You've got to teach me how to fly fish for trout." He paused, then added, "If you don't, I'm ruined."

I was shocked and showed it. The oyster slipped off the fork and plopped into the horse radish sauce.

"If you're going to ask how I can be the son of George Baldwin Potter and not know how to fish," he growled, "don't."

I had been about to ask. I didn't. Instead I ate an oyster.

"But why *do* you want to take up trout fishing?" I said.

"Want to!" he burst out. "Want to! I hate the very idea of fishing. But I've got to learn." He stopped, then looked wildly about. "And by this Saturday."

It was now Monday noon.

Potter was plainly a desperate man.

"Look," he continued on as I stared at him. "I'll explain it all. I have to learn to fish because I have to fish this weekend with an old guy named Aaron Alexander McPherson. If I can't fish he'll think I'm a creep and that'll be the end of Sally and me."

I looked at him blankly.

"Sally—Sally Winslow," he blundered on. "My fiancée, or, well—almost." He studied his plate for a moment. "And it's sort of your fault—your father's anyhow. Because he wrote all those stories about my father, and old McPherson read them."

"Maybe you'd better start at the beginning," I said. And he took me at my word.

"On my ninth birthday," George Baldwin Potter III began, "my father gave me a trout rod. For weeks I had begged for a model sailboat." He took a sip of water to calm himself.

"My father put it together for me. He had a little black reel for it and line that he stuck through those little wire things." ("Guides," I put in gently.) 'Son,' he said, putting his hand on my head. 'This is a three-and-three-eights-ounce Spinoza. Handle it gently and you'll be able to fish it all your life.'

"I said something like 'Gee, thanks, Dad.' And began looking around for the boat. Of course there wasn't any boat. Finally I asked, 'Is there a sailboat?' And I started to blubber. You know how kids are. The old man didn't say anything. He took the rod apart and put the pieces into the little green bag and slid the bag into its metal tube and went out of the room."

And so, as the meal progressed, George unreeled the painful story of a life blasted by fishing. From his earliest childhood his father, his father's friends, even people he met casually who had read his father's stories, expected him to be a passionate angler.

At first he tried. But he was big, clumsy, slow afoot. Flailing a trout stream with three-and-three-eighth ounces of skinny bamboo wasn't for him. He worked hard at other sports. At Yale he even won a major Y. But to his father none of this mattered. George was not a fisherman.

Such wounds heal, of course. In time he discovered there is a whole world of people who figure that a Light Cahill must be some kind of a pipe, and a 5X tippet something a pretty woman might wear to a Gay Nineties party. He got a job. He took up golf and sailing. He built a kind of life, untouched by the curse of fly fishing.

Then he met Sally. At her name his face turned bright and dreamy. "But," he continued sadly, "it was the old trout-fishing routine all over again."

"Sally fishes," I guessed, hoping to move things along.

"Oh, it's not her fault," Potter put in. The trouble, it appeared, was not Sally's fishing but her guardian, one Aaron Alexander McPherson, the Ball Bearing King. Even I had heard of McPherson. It was said of him that he used to finish off his ball bearings by personally grinding them down with his back teeth. It was also said that he kept a dwarf in his employ so that when anyone made a business pitch to him, he could bring on the dwarf and say, "Let's hear what the little people have to say."

"You see," said George. "McPherson promised Sally's father on his death bed, or some such, that he'd take care of the girl. He holds his money in trust till she's twenty-five."

"And he doesn't approve of you?" I asked.

"He doesn't approve of anybody," said George. "When I first went there he was barely civil. Talked about how lazy young men are today. Said the country needs hungry young go-getters—like he was. Then, just as I was about to go, my name suddenly struck a bell. 'George Baldwin Potter,' he said. Did I know the man in the stories? And naturally Sally told him that the Potter in the stories was real, and that I am his son. Right away he acted halfway human. Invited me up to the Castle next week for—fishing!"

"This is none of my business," I said, "but what do you need McPherson's blessing for. That's pretty antique stuff. Why not just get married?"

"That's what I wanted!" George exploded. "I've got no use for the guy's cash, or Sally's. But she won't do it without the old monster's approval. She calls him 'Uncle Alec' and says it would break his 'poor old' heart. That he really loves her, and stuff like that. But if I do all right at the Castle, she thinks he'll say okay. He's insane about fly fishing. Anyway," George concluded glumly, "we're set to fly to the Castle this Friday night."

I thought guardians had pretty much gone out with the passenger pigeon. Sally whatever-her-name-was didn't sound any too bright, either. But Potter's adoration was real. Maybe it was the gleam in George's eye whenever he spoke of the girl. Maybe it was the fairy-tale idiocy of the whole thing. But, without saying so, I realized that I'd agreed to help.

And there was no time at all. In four days George would not only have to learn to throw and retrieve a fly, net fish, and so on, but give *some* account of himself at the dinner table. A whirlwind campaign was in order.

For starters I dragged him off to my house in exurbia where there was some lawn to throw line on. Mornings and evenings—before and after commuting—we practiced casting. At night, and on the train, we could talk and he could read. Before I knew it I was in deeper than I planned. Sally told McPherson that George was with me. Through her the old man insisted that I come to the Castle, too. George leapt pitifully at the chance for some support, and I was hooked.

At dawn on Tuesday he and I rolled out onto the dew-drenched grass. Earnestly flailing the air, he tried to pause a beat at ten and two on an imaginary clockface, practicing a cast from near the back steps to the sundial half way across the lawn. An audience began to gather: our black lab Gumboots, Grisbi the cat, finally the three children. Grisbi fiercely studied the twitchy tip of George's line as he retrieved it. Gumboots watched Grisbi.

For a while these goings-on kept the kids quietly intent. But nothing stays simple.

"Daddy?" our three-year-old Carla called out.

"What is it baby?" I said patiently, watching George thrust his arm forward like a policeman about to pound on a door.

"Daddy," Carla continued with the serpentlike innocence of the very young, "does the man think there are fish in the garden?"

"No, baby" I said. "Mr. Potter is learning how to cast. And if you aren't quiet you'll all go in the house."

"Don't send them in," said George. "They're no bother. And they're probably a lot kinder about my casting than old man McPherson will be."

Then I had an idea. "I think you've had enough casting for now, George. Let's try playing a fish." Summoning Carla, I tied the line to the back of her belt. Then, putting the other two children at two sides of the lawn I told them: "You're both rocks. Big rocks, in the middle of the river. Carla's going to be a trout. She's going to run around and be pulled back by Mr. Potter."

I shooed dog and cat off the grass and signalled George to be ready. "Now Carla," I said, "run up and down the lawn. Sometimes run toward Mr. Potter. Sometimes run away from him."

At first it went fine. Carla churned up and down the lawn. When she headed toward George he obediently stripped in line as fast as he could. When she went away he gave line as slowly as he could, pulling on Carla and putting as much strain on rod and line as he dared.

Then catastrophe struck.

Grisbi dashed forward. Gumboots galumphed after him, banging into the "trout" and knocking her down. Howling, Carla scrambled to her feet and, with the retriever frolicking after her, set out at top speed for the end of the yard. George's reel screamed as the line unwound. "Stop!" I shouted. "Stop, Carla! He won't hurt you."

Too late. Carla's thirty-eight pounds of terrified flesh disappeared through my neighbor's cedar hedge. George was using, yes, that 3⅜-ounce Spinoza his father had given him long ago. "There it goes," I thought. But just after Carla got out of sight, the line, an old one I'd lent him, snapped off right where the end of the double taper had been knotted quickly to the reel.

We went in to breakfast.

"Hello," said my nonfishing wife cheerily. "How's the fishing?"

"Not bad," said my eldest son who had deigned to impersonate one of the rocks, "but you should have seen the one that got away."

Even after several days' practice, George's casting still put you in mind of a rusty tin soldier. He seemed to have so many muscles that it was impossible for him to let the rod do any of the work. We had naturally decided that he would have to present himself as the kind of fisherman who uses only a few fly patterns and works fast water with a short line. The Castle's waters were legendary for good trout. If now and then he could get his fly near where he wanted it and keep it afloat even for a second or two, he stood a chance of getting fish.

But as a potential fisherman George had another handicap. He was truthful to a fault, and he did not like to talk about fishing. Reading was more congenial. Fishing had already created so deep and painful an impression on George that I kept the fare light. No George M. L. LaBranche. No Dame Juliana Berners. No Edward Ringwood Hewitt. And, where possible, story-telling rather than instruction. This all took place long ago, in a simpler time when, for instance, the idea of fishing a nymph upstream with a greased leader was a dramatic innovation. Before William Humphrey's *The Spawning Run*. Before Norman Maclean's *A River Runs Through It*. I gave him some good stuff, though. Small doses of Roderick Haig-Brown, Frederick White's *The Spicklefisherman*, Arthur Train's wonderful story about how Ephraim Tutt got revenge on the WANIC Club.

George's questions about them were disconcerting.

"They're good stories," he commented, raising his head from the book as the 6:40 jiggled and rumbled us home on Thursday night. "But it beats me how all these grown men can take this fishing stuff seriously."

Friday morning he asked about Isaak Walton.

"Most people haven't actually read Walton," I explained. "They only know about him for talk. Walton was an ironmonger by trade. He called trout 'trouts,' and clergymen 'fishers of souls.' His wife wrote the doxology 'Praise God from whom all blessings flow.' Walton liked pretty milkmaids. He was dead set against chub."

"What's chub?" asked George.

What Aaron Alexander McPherson referred to as "The Castle" turned out to be a tract of land somewhat larger than the state of Rhode Island, tucked away in a corner of the Adirondacks. The whole place took its name from the cavernous stone pile that served McPherson as summer headquarters, a building that had originally stood on a hill not far from Loch Ness in the Scottish Highlands, where McPherson was born. One day when he was "nowt but a puir Scots lad wi' a mean temper," as we heard the story, the laird's men caught him trying to snag trout out of castle waters.

They were foolish enough to thrash the lad and drag him before the laird, who then publicly ran him off the place.

Six months later McPherson set sail for America. Fifteen years after that, by then already the ball-bearing king, he sailed back, bought the castle and had it shipped—stone by stone—to upstate New York where it had sat ever since, as ugly and damp as ever it had been in Scotland, but sheer balm to the revengeful soul of the ball-bearing king.

George and I were the last guests to arrive. Standing in front of the great fireplace was our host, and right away I figured the story about the dwarf and the "little people" had to be a base canard; he stood barely as tall as my ten-year-old son. In other respects, though, Mc-

Pherson was the perfect caricature of a mean Scotsman, with a narrow, wizened face that seemed to have done time in a bottle of formaldehyde, little tufts of white hair curling from his ears, shaggy eyebrows over close-set, glittery eyes sighted in past a modified Mount Rushmore nose.

His greeting was cordial, however, and for a moment I was reassured. Over drinks on a terrace overlooking the Fario, the name McPherson had given his stream, we learned that it was divided into eight fishing beats, each lavishly stocked with big brown trout. McPherson described with relish how he'd dispossessed the laird and brought the castle "over the water," and how he snapped up the land and the river by beating out a distant relative of Jay Gould's.

The water we would be fishing, apparently, had the usual legendary monster trout. It lay in a deep pool not far from the Castle in Beat 1, a brown trout so big nobody could be sure just how big it was, though there were the customary tales of how it had been seen by this one or that one, simply inhaling a baby squirrel or gulping down the occasional duckling. For miles around, we learned, this creature was known as the Loch Ness Monster, a name McPherson had bestowed on the fish, apparently without fear that the locals might apply it to anything besides the trout.

The old man's face was tense as he told how this great trout had defied him, smashing his tackle, breaking one of his rods, ignoring the costliest flies that money could buy. Even laying a fly over the Monster was complicated. He customarily lay under a bank in the widest and deepest pool on the river. Explaining it, McPherson at first arranged books and pieces of bric-a-brac on a table, then, losing patience, he actually whisked us away from our drinks by jeep so we could see what he was talking about.

Standing above the river it was easy to sympathize with our host, who now began to discourse with the passion of a general overlooking a once and future battlefield. From the side we were on, the Castle side, it was clear the fish could not be reached with a dry fly at all—the water was too deep to wade and the bank, except for one open space, was too thick with small birch trees to allow a backcast. Even on the shallow far side, most of the pool was unwadable.

In fact, the only way to throw a fly over the Monster was to work your way from the far shore down a long, narrow gravel bar that angled downstream into the pool and take a stand on a submerged rock at the end of it. The rock was about fifty feet from the Castle side of the river. By casting across current and a bit upstream you could just barely reach the fish. For someone as small as McPherson, I saw, that would be a ticklish thing. The current, from a waterfall at the head of the pool, was strong. Even standing on the rock, McPherson told us, the water was nearly up to his wader tops.

Not that this deterred him. "I tell you, laddie," he shouted to George above the rush of the river below us," I'll have yon Monster yet." His eyes gleamed under those tufted brows—and right then I would not have switched places with that trout for all the caddisflies in Christendom.

The thought of the great trout and, even more, the sight of a stream had given me (as it always does) what today is called a high. Back at the Castle where drinks continued, I winked at George, and whispered, "piece of cake." It seemed to me that even my Aunt Matilda, a bedridden ninety-one, could not fail to catch fish in the Fario.

Then McPherson began explaining to his eleven guests just how they would spend their next two days.

What he had arranged was something truly ghastly—a fishing contest. We would be divided into two teams and fish in pairs, the pairings and the beats each pair fished to be switched every day. A flock of jeeps driven by Castle staff would whisk us to and fro like clockwork, so that no one had more stream time than anyone else. By McPherson's decree no fish under fourteen inches could be killed, and no fisherman could take more than five fish a day. Dry flies were de rigueur.

All that was bad enough. Even worse, it appeared that this year's contest was a grudge fight. One team was to be led by McPherson himself, the other by a tall, cold-eyed dutchman with a name that sounded like Count van Workhorse. Apparently these contests were a Castle tradition, and the Count—that was how McPherson invariably referred to him—had been outfishing the old man for years. Announcing the scoring system—extra prizes and points for individuals and teams with the heaviest fish—and the heaviest total catch—our host made reference to his rival's former victories.

"The Count should take warning," he concluded ominously. "This year may be a different story." And he glanced fleetingly toward George and me. We were both on his team. In one sickening instant I realized that he had brought us in as supposed ringers.

It was a grisly prospect that seemed to spell ruin for George and Sally's hopes. For a moment or two I gave some deep thought to the subject of worms; McPherson's contest, after all, clearly deserved no quarter. Then I remembered all those jeep drivers zipping up and down the river and nobly put such ideas behind me.

The only bright spot in the dismal evening that followed was Sally Winslow. Blonde and brown-eyed, she was as willowy as George's ancient Spinoza, as trim (reader forgive me) as a new-tied number-18 Pink Lady. Despite being so decorative, she seemed to be the kind of girl who might be able to camp out without complaint, or work a small boat to windward in a driving rain without worrying about her hairdo. My estimation of George's taste, as well as my devotion to his cause, rocketed accordingly. Sally had been assigned to our team, but I noticed that the Count joined the rest of us in flocking to her like teenage moths around a flame.

The dawn of the first day was sunny. A small fleet of jeeps bounced us to our battle stations. I was paired that morning on Beat 4 with a leathery lady called Mrs. Whitebait (or Lightwait). George was to share Beat 8 with the Count.

"Piece of cake!" he muttered as we waited for our jeeps. "I feel like a man walking the last mile."

"Cheer up," I said with a heartiness I was far from feeling. "This stream is packed with big trout. Keep clear of the pools and you'll do all right."

Under other circumstances this would have been a moment of pure joy, for the Fario, slicing down out of the hills, turned out to be a stream pretty enough to make poets of peasants. It ran against a rocky ridge, following it down through a succession of narrow valleys. It was deep and shadowy on the ridge side, slipping over shale rock sprinkled with boulders and overhung by hemlocks.

On the other side it shallowed and was bordered by small meadows and grassy banks. Surprisingly narrow, it had the appearance of a small stream. The Little Beaverkill comes to mind, but with a lot more water, a current that ran heavy and often deep, so fast and deep in fact that only here and there could you wade across it. McPherson had put up a half dozen swinging foot bridges so he and his guests could get from the deep side—where the Castle stood—to the shallow side, from which the stream could be most easily fished.

It should have been a delirious day. Hardly had I cast a number-16 Dark Hendrickson upon the waters than I began to catch fish more readily than I ever had before—except for trips in the far north that don't count, trout up there never having heard of people. I soon saw, though, that McPherson's fourteen-inch keeping rule and his scoring systems created an unexpected problem: not how to take fish, but what fish to take.

If you killed fourteen-inch fish you would soon have your limit and be out of action for the day. Clearly, logic said to ease them back into the stream and wait for much heavier game. But how much heavier? And how long should you wait? The Fario clearly had plenty of underwater food and, heaven knows, even on an overstocked, underfished dream stream, trout can suddenly start exercising their inalienable right to be picky—especially where dry flies are concerned. Reckoning that thinking big was the only way for our side to win—and so keep McPherson's disapproval from falling upon George—I released fish after fish. And switched to larger and larger flies.

The plan seemed to work. By lunchtime, when jeeps came to collect us, I had an eighteen-inch brown and a seventeen-inch rainbow, whose presence in these waters startled me a bit but whose high-flying helped me forget that I was nothing but a pot hunter. Back at the Castle I was happy to find I'd figured the odds, if not right, at least with the experts. Both the Count and McPherson had kept only two trout, about the size and weight of mine. Even George had two fourteen-inch browns. These were his first fish; the poor fellow felt quite set up. But as we went into lunch I could see our side was already a bit behind—and by the margin of George's catch. McPherson clearly noticed it too.

Lunch, served outdoors by the stream, was lavish: cold salmon flown in from Cape Breton, and Pouilly Fuissé chilled in an icy mountain spring, followed by strawberries and champagne. Still, it was a far from festive meal. McPherson glowered. The Count gloated. Besides paying marked attention to Sally, he seemed to feel the need to provide us all with a stream-of-consciousness, fly-by-fly, and rise-by-rise account of his day on the stream. George, beside Mrs. Lightwait (or Whitebait) glumly toyed with his salmon and tried to avoid making any piscatorial gaffs. It seemed an age until the arrival of coffee released us for another go at the stream.

The rest of the weekend I had what should have been the greatest trout fishing of my life. But firmly fixed in the notion that killing big fish was the only way to ward off disaster for George and Sally, I turned what should have been a pleasure into a grim and bloody job. Deer appeared in the fields beside me but I had no time to look at them. A mink came slipping downstream toward me, only the third I'd seen in years of fishing, but instead of freezing to watch him, I went right on casting, and even felt a twinge of resentment. He was after my fish!

Instead of enjoying the runs and jumps of trout I had on, I was shaken by a feverish fear that they might get off, and horsed them in as hard as my tackle would stand. I was tense, rather than intent, and, when working flat water, found myself striking too early any time I even glimpsed a fish, something I had not done since I was a boy.

McPherson's team fell steadily behind. George did his best. But his time on the water was often spent trying to extract his fly from overhanging branches or, worse, unsnarling his leader. Once, tightening the leader tippet as he clumsily tied on a fly, his hand slipped, driving the barb of a Cahill well into his thumb. All his rage and frustration at the weekend focused on this mishap and, seizing his fly scissors, he savagely cut the hook out. "It was either that or have everybody hear about it," he said when he told me the story later. I stood speechless, staring at the gash in his finger.

Saturday dinner in the huge dining hall was funereal. Ominously, George had been moved from his place of honor beside McPherson, and sat far down the table. The Count had taken his place. Rain blasted down on the Castle in sheets. Marking it, the Count called out cheerily: "Rising river tomorrow, Alex. Rising river, rising fish." But McPherson only responded, "Aye," and sourly poked at his roast beef.

Sitting with downcast eyes in that baronial setting, George and Sally looked like a pair of star-crossed Renaissance lovers. It was the first time I had seen Sally depressed, so I was not surprised when, on my way upstairs, I found her waiting for me on the landing.

"Those knights of old who endured ordeals of self-denial and tests of courage for their lady loves," I said, "have nothing on old George."

"Poor George," she sighed. "I got him into this. But I had no idea it would turn out this way."

I grunted.

"No, really," she said. "I hadn't. You see, Uncle Alec, however he seems to you, loves me. He usually gives me what I want and he knows I want George. But he's so grim now, I just don't know what will happen."

I thought I knew all too well.

"All it takes with Uncle Alec," Sally pursued, "is some little spark of approval. But he's just crazy about this competition thing."

"Cheer up," I said. "There's always fisherman's luck." At this lame offering, she gave me a woeful you've-got-to-be-kidding look, and turned away.

The next day I quit the stream early, before noon in fact. Though I had taken some notable trout, I had given up on the fishing match. What our side needed was something, well, something truly monstrous. We had a half day of fishing still to go, of course. But barring some sort of riverside miracle, of the kind that, in my experience, only occur in fishing stories, we would never catch up with the Count's team.

George's beat was next to mine. Heading back, I stepped upstream along the bank toward the foot of Beat 5, where he had been assigned to fish. To my astonishment I found him not in fast water as we had agreed, but at the foot of a long, glassy pool. It was one of those rare spots where the Fario flattens and shallows. When I came on him George was standing in about ten inches of water, flabbily casting toward a big, flat rock three rod lengths above him. It was bright sunlight. The Count's predicted rain had come and gone, though more was expected at lunch time.

George was a dismaying sight. His rod tip was down. His line, looping around on the water above him, needed drying and greasing. His leader lay in a sickening S-loop on the pool's surface. Attached to it was an enormous Fanwing Royal Coachman.

"George!" I shouted. "What are you doing?"

He was committing the act of casting when I called. He waited until the still face of the pool had shuddered under the impact of his line, leader, and fly, which fluttered to the water wings down, then turned toward me.

"There was some splashing down here," he said guiltily. "And I wasn't doing any good up above."

"Well," I said smugly, "you've got about as much chance of getting fish here as you would in the Information Booth of Grand Central."

Before George could answer there was a sort of explosion up beside the rock where his hapless fanwing lay. Nothing more startling than a five-inch shell would have made, but not anything you could easily overlook.

"Strike!" I yelled. By the time I said it the advice was superfluous. Whatever had caused the splash had taken the fly, hooked itself, and was now heading in the general direction of Montreal.

"After him!" I shouted. But George was already stumbling upstream. Near the top of the pool the fish broke water, turned in the air, and chunked back with a full-bodied splash. It was a huge brown trout. Since we were not in Beat 1 I knew this wasn't the Loch Ness Monster, but just that glimpse of him made me weak in the legs.

With George tagging behind, the fish hit the fast water above the pool at high speed, charged up it almost to the pool above. At the top of the run it seemed to stay motionless, holding its own against the pressure from rod and rapids. Then it tore back down into the pool where it had been hooked. George stripped in line like a veteran.

After sulking in the deep water near my side of the stream, the trout swung in a short arc above George and jumped again.

"I can't feel him anymore," George called.

I started to yell, "Get more line in," when George shouted, "Through my legs!" And he lurched sideways to clear his line. Still on, the fish flashed straight down the pool while George was getting his balance. This was the end, I knew. Once into the fast water below there'd be no stopping it.

But we were lucky. At the end of its downstream run the big fish checked, turned aside, and bored under a rock—the same rock, in fact, near which he'd been hooked. We were still in the game.

"George," I called. "Take it easy. You've got to get him headed away from those rapids. Come quietly down the edge of the pool so as not to scare him. When you get below the rock, wade up toward it and try to kick him out upstream."

Obediently, George clumped down the shallow rim of the pool. Every step he took I expected the fish to blast off downstream. But it lay quiet. Finally, what seemed an hour later, George was in place. He splashed toward the rock. The line moved upstream.

The fight was on again.

George hung in there nobly. And eventually the fish began to come his way. It drifted at last into shallow water. While I kept up a steady chatter of instructions, it was drawn nearer and nearer. Slowly and carefully, George backed toward shore. Slowly and carefully he groped around for his net handle. Just watching him I found I could hardly breathe.

It seemed as if the sport of fishing had at long last done the right thing by George Baldwin Potter III. The impossible had occurred. Victory was in sight. But then, as I am told it so often does on the great stream of life, disaster struck. Shuffling backward George turned an ankle on a small boulder, lost his balance, pawed at the air with his empty net, and sat down in the pool. The exhausted trout thrashed in the shallow water. On his back George lunged for it with the net. Too late. The great fish wearily glided out into the dark pool, taking with him our last hope of success.

The sun was setting over the river as my driver braked his jeep by the Castle. Our competition was over. That last afternoon a brief but heavy cloud-burst at the headwaters of the Fario had finally put the stream on a sharp rise. It had brought good fishing. I was late, though, not because I lingered after trout but because I wanted to put off as long as I could the final reckoning of our contest and old McPherson's world-class disappointment. By some grotesque irony the drawn lots had paired George with McPherson himself on Beat 1 for this, the final afternoon of fishing. Under the glittering eye of Sally Winslow's guardian there was no telling what grief George might have come to.

But when I joined the others neither George nor the old man was there. Most of the guests were checking in their creels with the Count, who was briskly keeping track of the score. Sally, however, was standing apart.

"I'm worried," she said as I came up. "Please. Let's get a jeep and get down to Beat 1." I didn't think anything more could be done for George, and just now the last thing I wanted was to tangle with McPherson. But I went with her.

Sally was certain we would find the old man in the Loch Ness Monster's pool. Sure enough, as our driver swung the jeep up to the stand of birch trees we glimpsed a dark figure in the middle of the river. We rushed to the bank. It was McPherson. The pool, as I've mentioned, was very broad just there, and the old man was nearer our shore than the one opposite—only about fifty feet from where we stood. The sinking sun behind him had turned him into a small, black silhouette but it was clear that he was up to his elbows in coiling water. And as we stared we could see that against his chest, barely out of water, he was clutching the biggest trout I've ever seen in my life.

"It's the Monster," Sally shrieked. "He's caught the Monster at last."

Just then McPherson saw us. Between his position and our shore the deepest, heaviest rush of the still-rising river swirled and eddied. His voice came to us faintly, muffled by the rumble of the waterfall at the pool's head.

"C-a-a-n-t get o-o-u-t," he called, adding something else that was lost in the rush of the waters.

"Drop the fish!" Sally called out, cupping her hands.

The old man shook his head. Even at that distance it was clear he would as soon give up his right leg as that trout.

McPherson's predicament was simple. Out to settle the score with the Loch Ness Monster he had ignored the rising water and worked his way down the narrow gravel bar and onto the rock at its tip so he could put a fly over the big fish's lair. Though the water was high on his waders, quartering downstream to get into position must have been comparatively easy. The current had helped.

God knows how he had landed the Monster. But now, burdened by a prize too vast to fit into creel or net, he couldn't fight his way back up the gravel bar. It looked to me, in fact, as if even without the trout, he might have a hard time beating a retreat. There was sharp risk of sliding off the gravel bar or, while struggling upstream with the current building against him, of filling his waders with water and being sucked away.

Sally had sent the jeep driver wheeling off to the nearest bridge, a mile and more away, so he could cross and rescue McPherson. Minutes passed. Just as I was beginning to think I'd have to strip off my boots and waders and try an icy dip in the pool, the bearlike figure of George Baldwin Potter rambled out of the underbrush across from us.

We could just make out that McPherson was shouting instructions. After a minute George began slowly lurching his way down the gravel bar. Big as he was he had a hard time of it. Once he lost his balance, and staggered for a second, wildly waving his arms. To me it looked as if in the process he'd shipped a good bit of water over the tops of his waders. But at last he stood beside the Ball Bearing King.

I did not envy George the sticky problem he now faced: how to maneuver an irascible old Scotsman who held the keys to his future happiness, *and* a slippery trout half as big as the Ritz, back through treacherous footing and heavy water. The old man alone would have been trouble enough. But it was clear that George must save the fish too. Could he possibly tuck the trout under one arm and still help Sally's guardian safely along the gravel bar with the other? Could he *carry* McPherson bodily, with the old man still grimly clutching the trout? Even as we watched we could see that they were both angrily arguing.

What happened next I will never forget. Before any of us could think what he was up to, George seized the Loch Ness Monster from McPherson's reluctant grasp and seemed to be twirling it around his head by the tail. Silhouetted there, it looked as big as a tuna. My heart sank. Something's snapped, I thought. George is going to let old McPherson have it, and with his own fish.

A second later the dark body of the giant trout separated from the figures of the two men in the river. Up it sailed, against the setting sun, and over the water, to fall with a tremendous, damp thump. There lay the Loch Ness Monster in the grass at Sally Winslow's feet.

McPherson and George arrived at the Castle a few moments after we got back in our jeep. The old man, jittering around like a terrier, waited for his fish to be weighed. As the scales were read he called out the result: "Seven pounds, ten ounces." It was more than enough, I knew, to win the match.

Sally ran to George and I followed.

"That was some heave," I growled with awe.

"Not so tough," he said. "That darned fish weighs about the same as a light shot."

Only then did the teasing memory that flickered in my mind when George had first mentioned his success on the track team come into focus. In his day, and mine, he had been a shot-put man—and one of the best in the country.

As I digested this thought, Aaron Alexander McPherson detached himself from his admiring guests and came toward us. I was afraid we were in for an account of his epic struggle with the Monster, but he simply held out his hand to George and thanked him warmly.

"You're no much of a hand at the catching of fish," he rumbled, with a stagey wink aside to Sally. "But when it comes to tossing 'em, laddie, you're in a class by yourself."